MORE PRAISE FOR BABYMOUSE!

"Sassy, smart . . . Babymouse is here to stay."
—The Horn Book Magazine

"Young readers will happily fall in line."
—Kirkus Reviews

"The brother-sister creative team hits the mark with humor, sweetness, and characters so genuine they can pass for real kids." —Booklist

"Babymouse is spunky, ambitious, and, at times, a total dweeb."
—School Library Journal

Be sure to read **all the BABYMOUSE** books:

#1 BABYMOUSE: Queen of the World!
#2 BABYMOUSE: Our Hero
#3 BABYMOUSE: Beach Babe
#4 BABYMOUSE: Rock Star
#5 BABYMOUSE: Heartbreaker
#6 CAMP BABYMOUSE
#7 BABYMOUSE: Skater Girl
#8 BABYMOUSE: Puppy Love
#9 BABYMOUSE: Monster Mash
#10 BABYMOUSE: The Musical

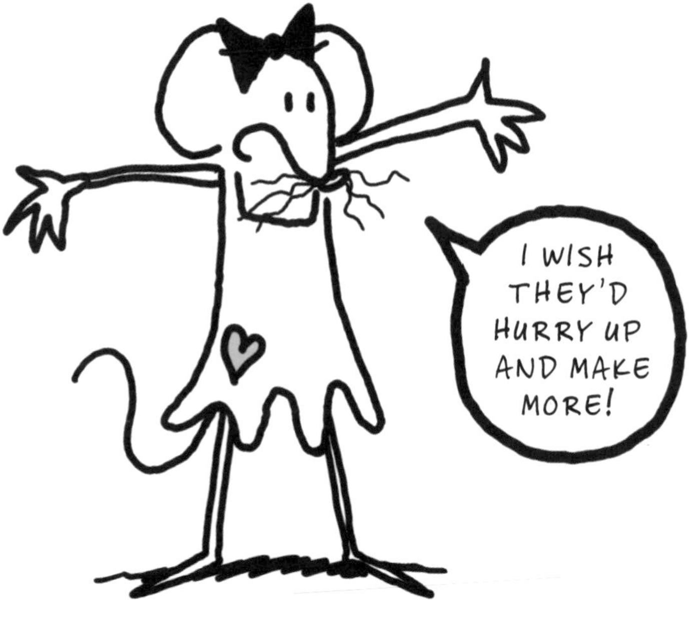
I WISH THEY'D HURRY UP AND MAKE MORE!

BABYMOUSE

ROCK STAR

BY JENNIFER L. HOLM & MATTHEW HOLM

RANDOM HOUSE 🏠 NEW YORK

BABYM♡USE WUZ HERE

HEE-HEE!

Copyright © 2006 by Jennifer Holm and Matthew Holm.

All rights reserved.
Published in the United States by Random House Children's Books, a division of Random House, Inc., New York.

RANDOM HOUSE and colophon are registered trademarks of Random House, Inc.

www.randomhouse.com/kids
www.babymouse.com

Educators and librarians, for a variety of teaching tools, visit us at www.randomhouse.com/teachers

Library of Congress Cataloging-in-Publication Data
Holm, Jennifer L.
Babymouse : rock star / Jennifer Holm and Matthew Holm.
    p. cm.
ISBN 978-0-375-83232-1 (trade) — ISBN 978-0-375-93232-8 (lib. bdg.)
I. Graphic novels. I. Holm, Matthew. II. Title.
PN6727.H592B34 2006
741.5'973—dc22
2005046464

MANUFACTURED IN MALAYSIA

14 13 12 11 10 9

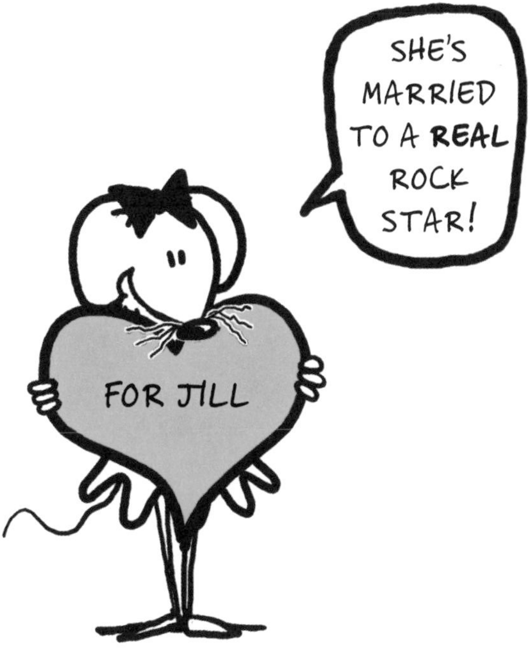
SHE'S MARRIED TO A **REAL** ROCK STAR!
FOR JILL

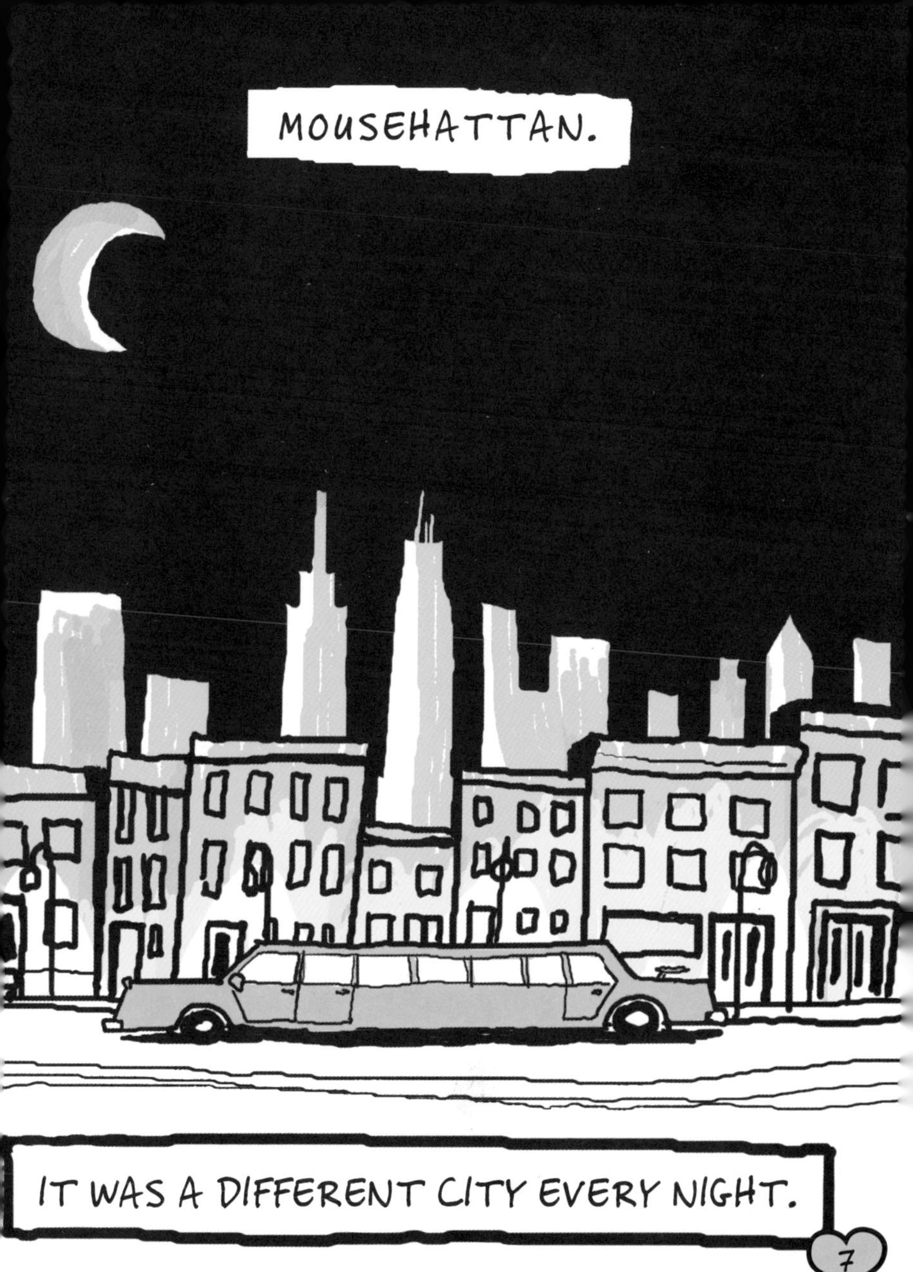
MOUSEHATTAN.
IT WAS A DIFFERENT CITY EVERY NIGHT.

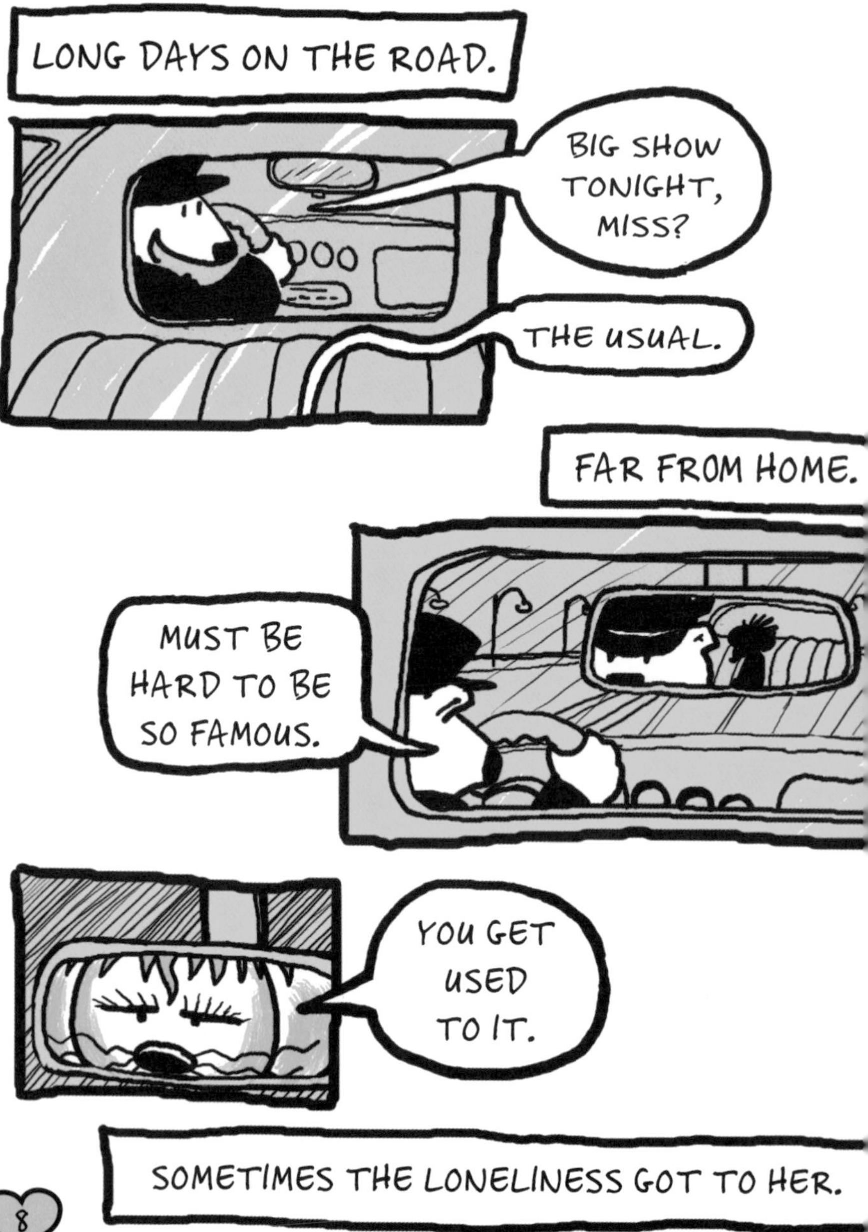
LONG DAYS ON THE ROAD.
BIG SHOW TONIGHT, MISS?
THE USUAL.
FAR FROM HOME.
MUST BE HARD TO BE SO FAMOUS.
YOU GET USED TO IT.
SOMETIMES THE LONELINESS GOT TO HER.

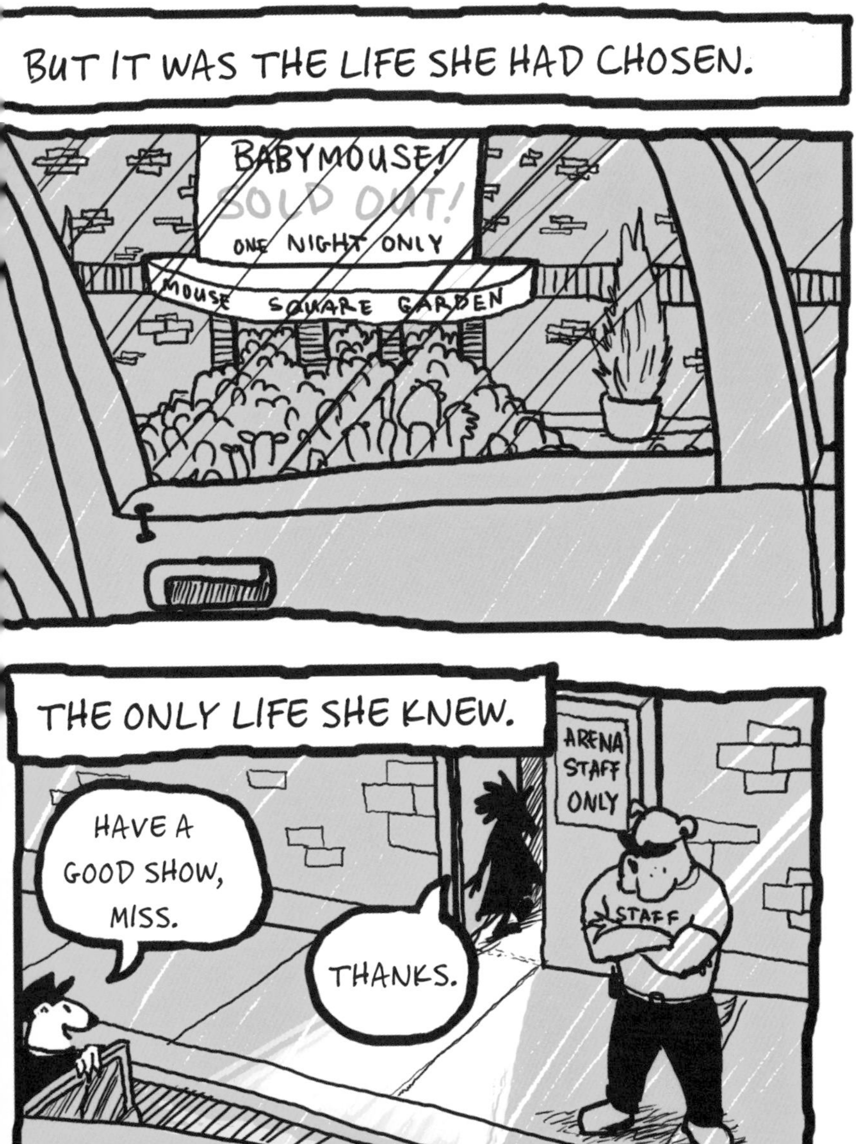
BUT IT WAS THE LIFE SHE HAD CHOSEN.
BABYMOUSE!
SOLD OUT!
ONE NIGHT ONLY
MOUSE SQUARE GARDEN
THE ONLY LIFE SHE KNEW.
ARENA STAFF ONLY
HAVE A GOOD SHOW, MISS.
THANKS.
STAFF

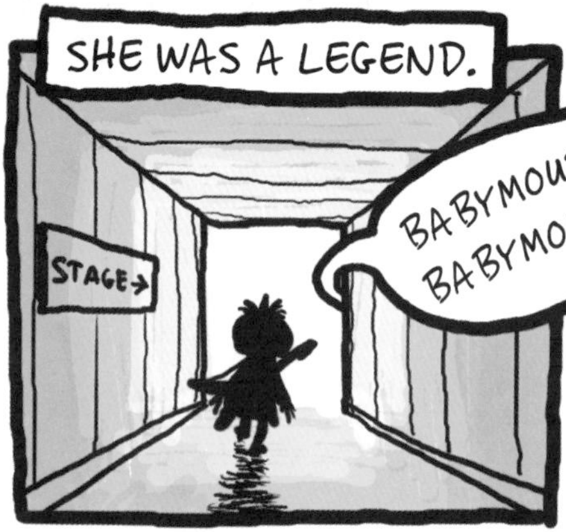
SHE WAS A LEGEND.
STAGE →
BABYMOUSE! BABYMOUSE!

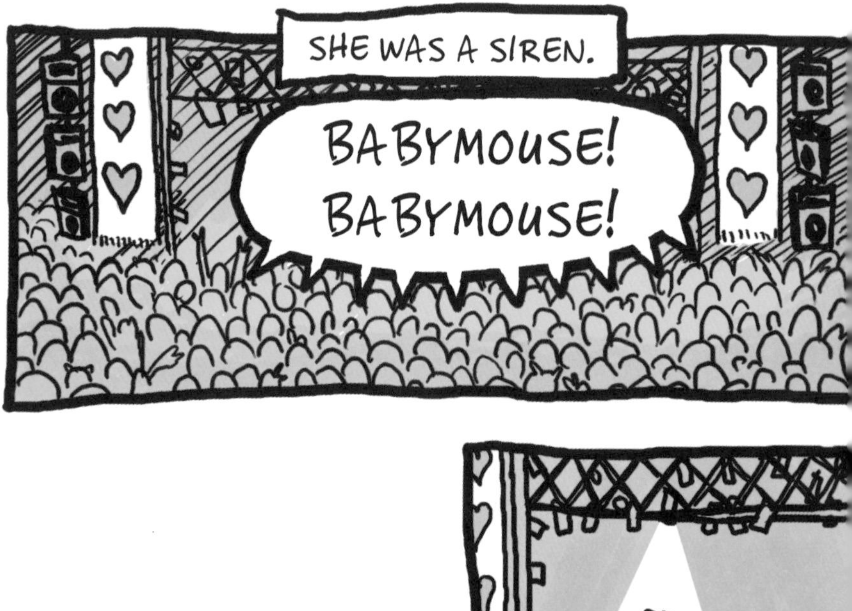
SHE WAS A SIREN.
BABYMOUSE! BABYMOUSE!

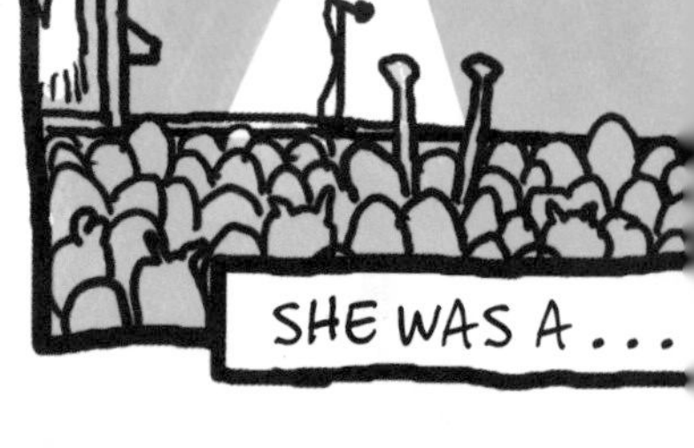
SHE WAS A . . .

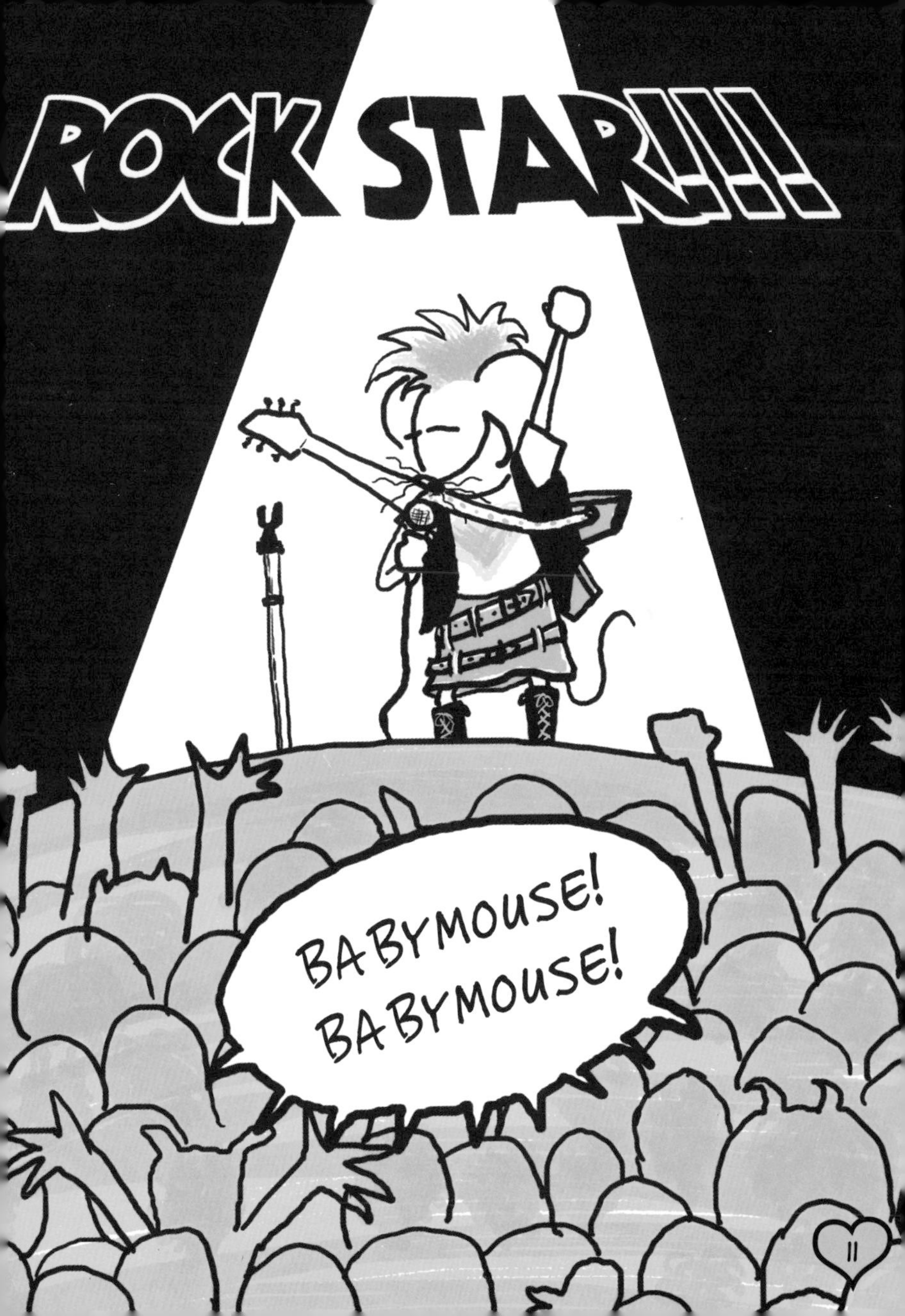
ROCK STAR!!!!
BABYMOUSE!
BABYMOUSE!

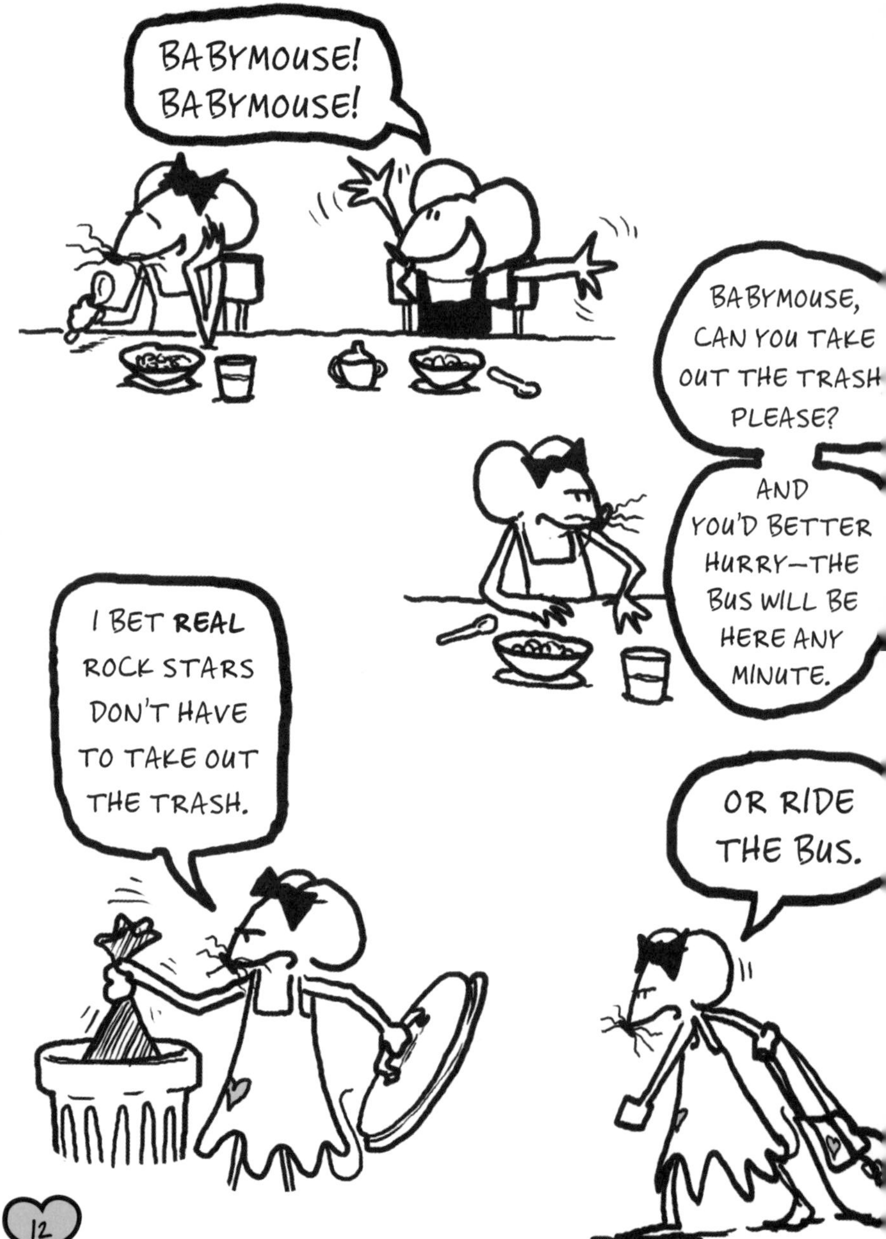
BABYMOUSE! BABYMOUSE!
BABYMOUSE, CAN YOU TAKE OUT THE TRASH PLEASE?
AND YOU'D BETTER HURRY—THE BUS WILL BE HERE ANY MINUTE.
I BET **REAL** ROCK STARS DON'T HAVE TO TAKE OUT THE TRASH.
OR RIDE THE BUS.

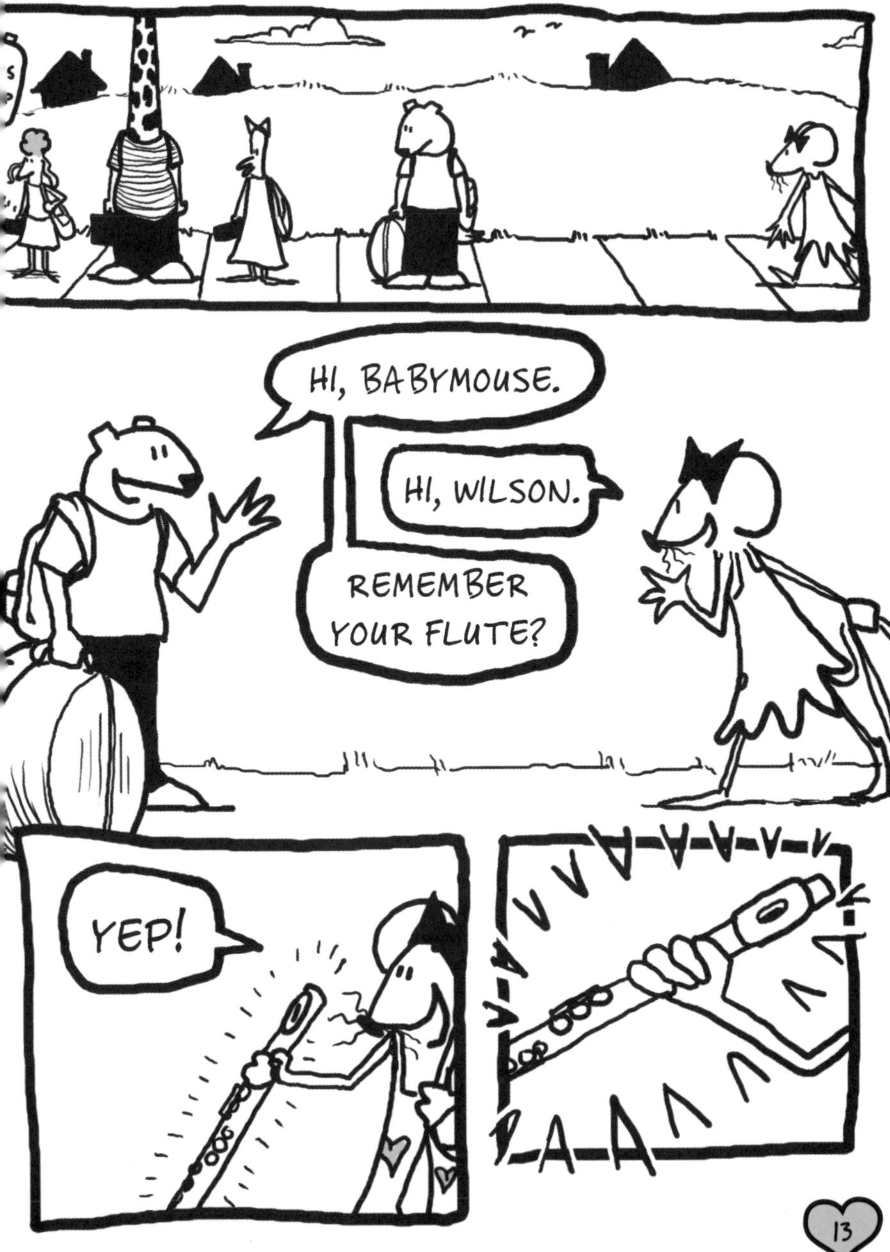
HI, BABYMOUSE.
HI, WILSON.
REMEMBER YOUR FLUTE?
YEP!

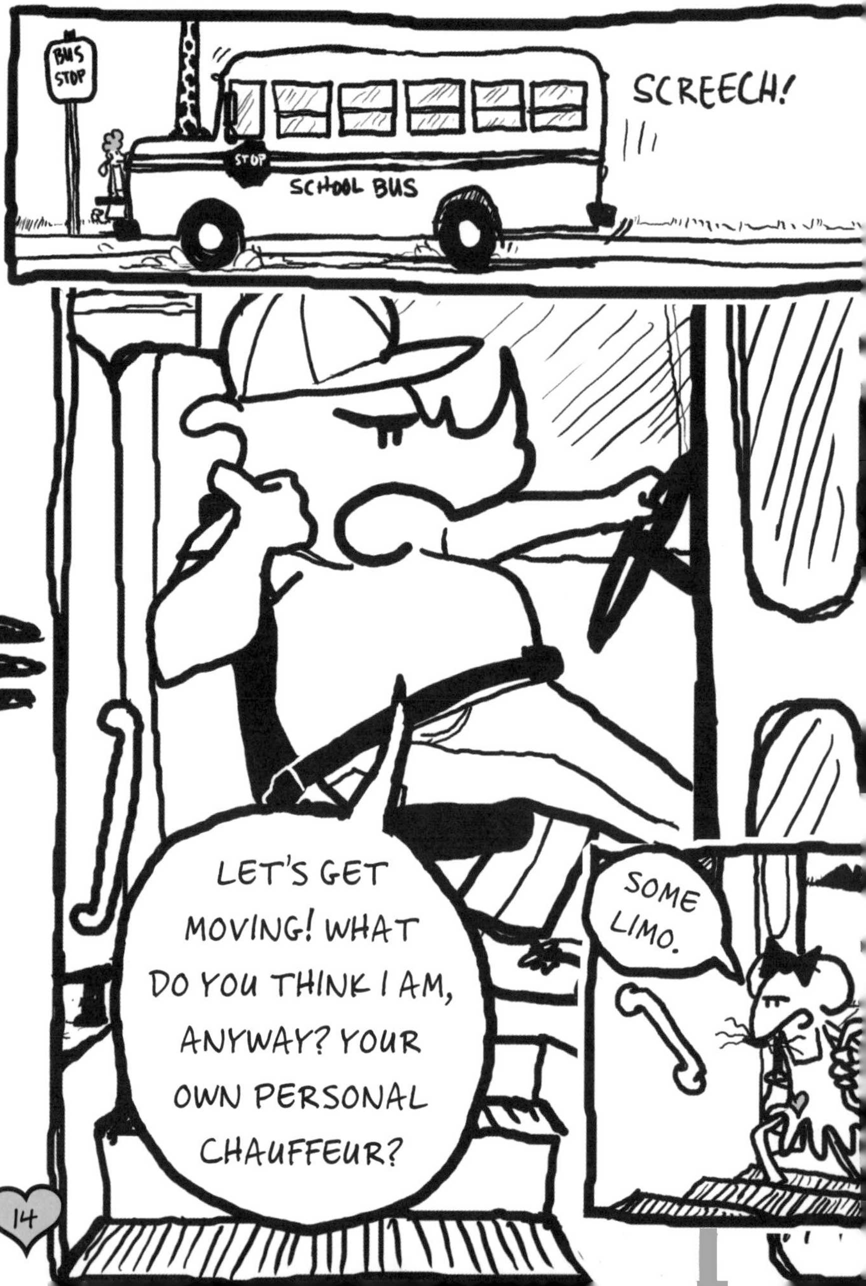
BUS STOP
STOP
SCHOOL BUS
SCREECH!
LET'S GET MOVING! WHAT DO YOU THINK I AM, ANYWAY? YOUR OWN PERSONAL CHAUFFEUR?
SOME LIMO.

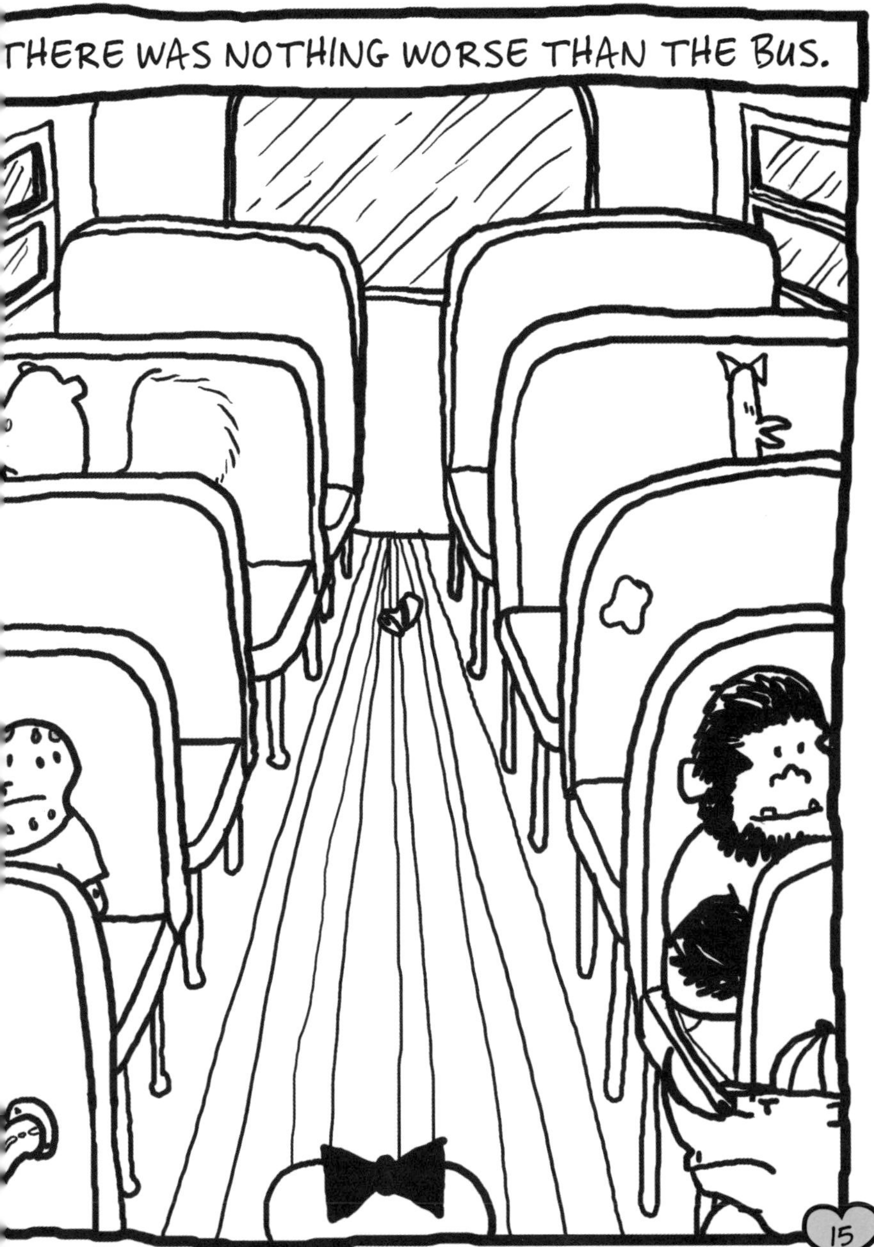
THERE WAS NOTHING WORSE THAN THE BUS.

IT WAS LIKE AN OBSTACLE COURSE.
DOESN'T OPEN
GETS BUS-SICK
TALKS TOO MUCH
SODA SPILL
GUM
BUMPY
RICKETY
KIND OF SCARY
PICKS NOSE
YELLS

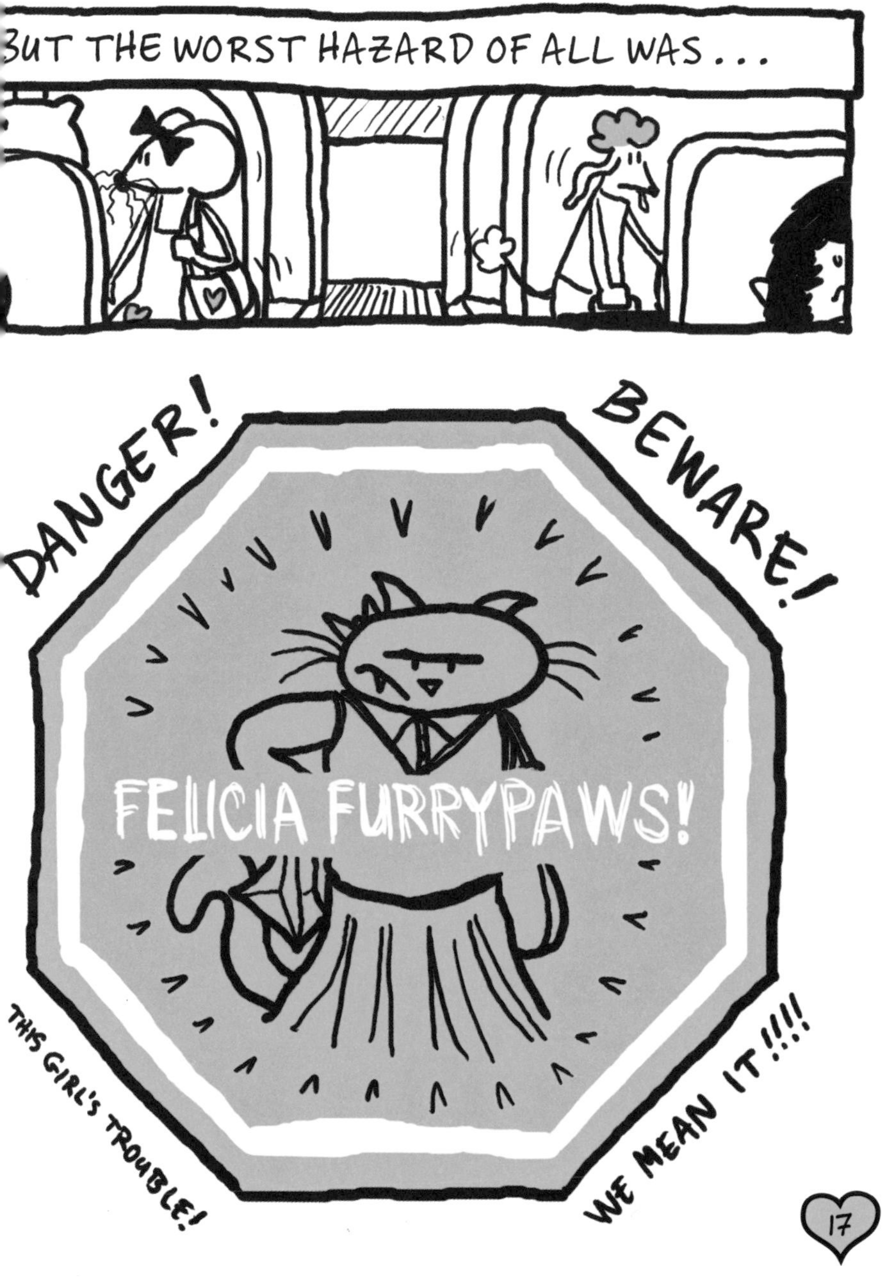

BUT THE WORST HAZARD OF ALL WAS...
DANGER!
BEWARE!
FELICIA FURRYPAWS!
THIS GIRL'S TROUBLE!
WE MEAN IT!!!!

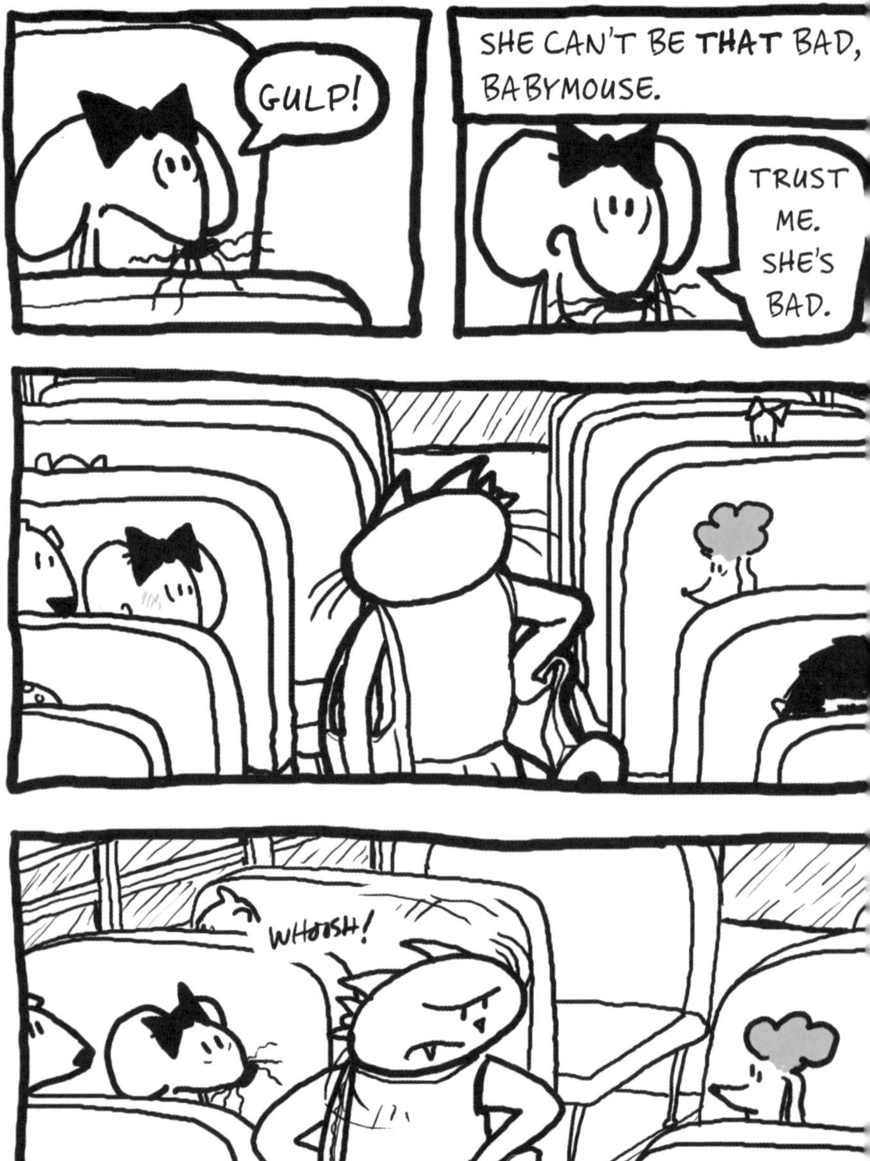
GULP!
SHE CAN'T BE **THAT** BAD, BABYMOUSE.
TRUST ME. SHE'S BAD.
WHOOSH!

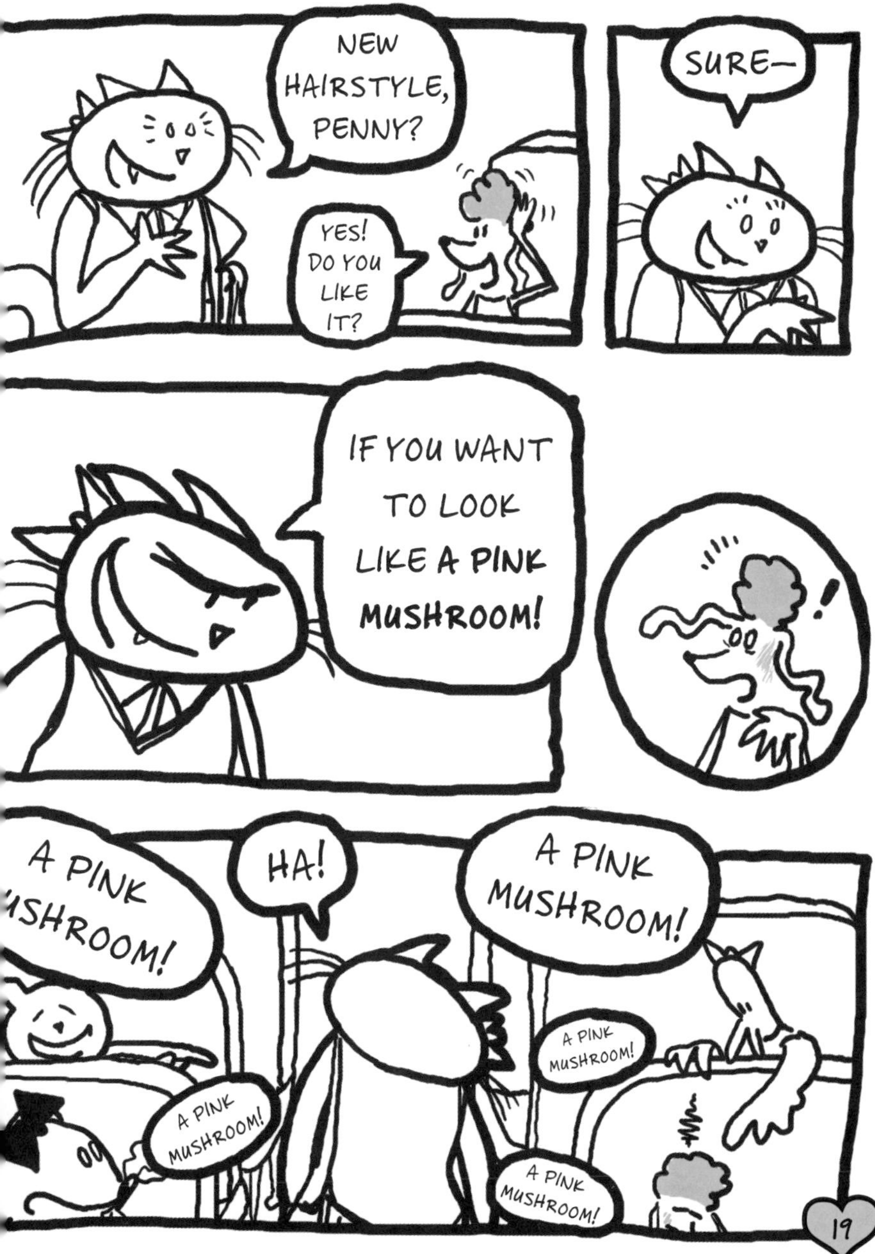

NEW HAIRSTYLE, PENNY?
YES! DO YOU LIKE IT?
SURE—
IF YOU WANT TO LOOK LIKE A PINK MUSHROOM!
!
A PINK MUSHROOM!
HA!
A PINK MUSHROOM!
A PINK MUSHROOM!
A PINK MUSHROOM!
A PINK MUSHROOM!

EXTRA! EXTRA! READ ALL ABOUT IT!
M NEWS

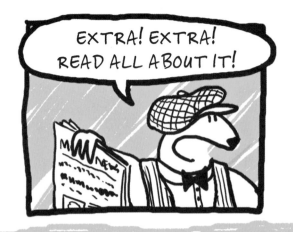

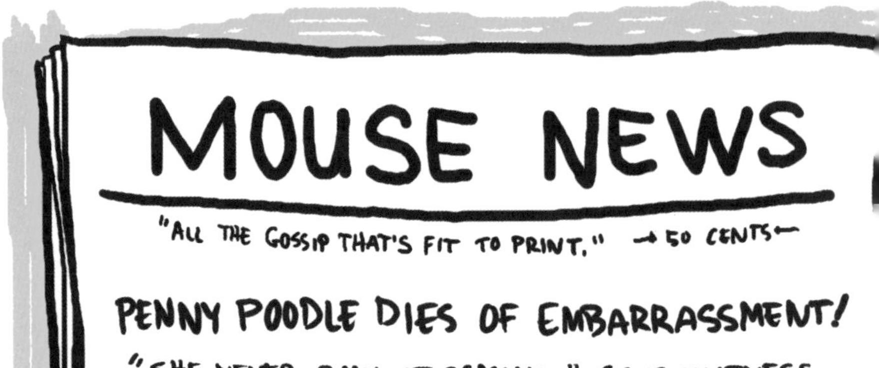

MOUSE NEWS
"ALL THE GOSSIP THAT'S FIT TO PRINT." →50 CENTS←
PENNY POODLE DIES OF EMBARRASSMENT!
"SHE NEVER SAW IT COMING," SAYS WITNESS.
PENNY POODLE

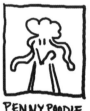

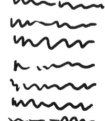

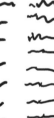

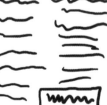

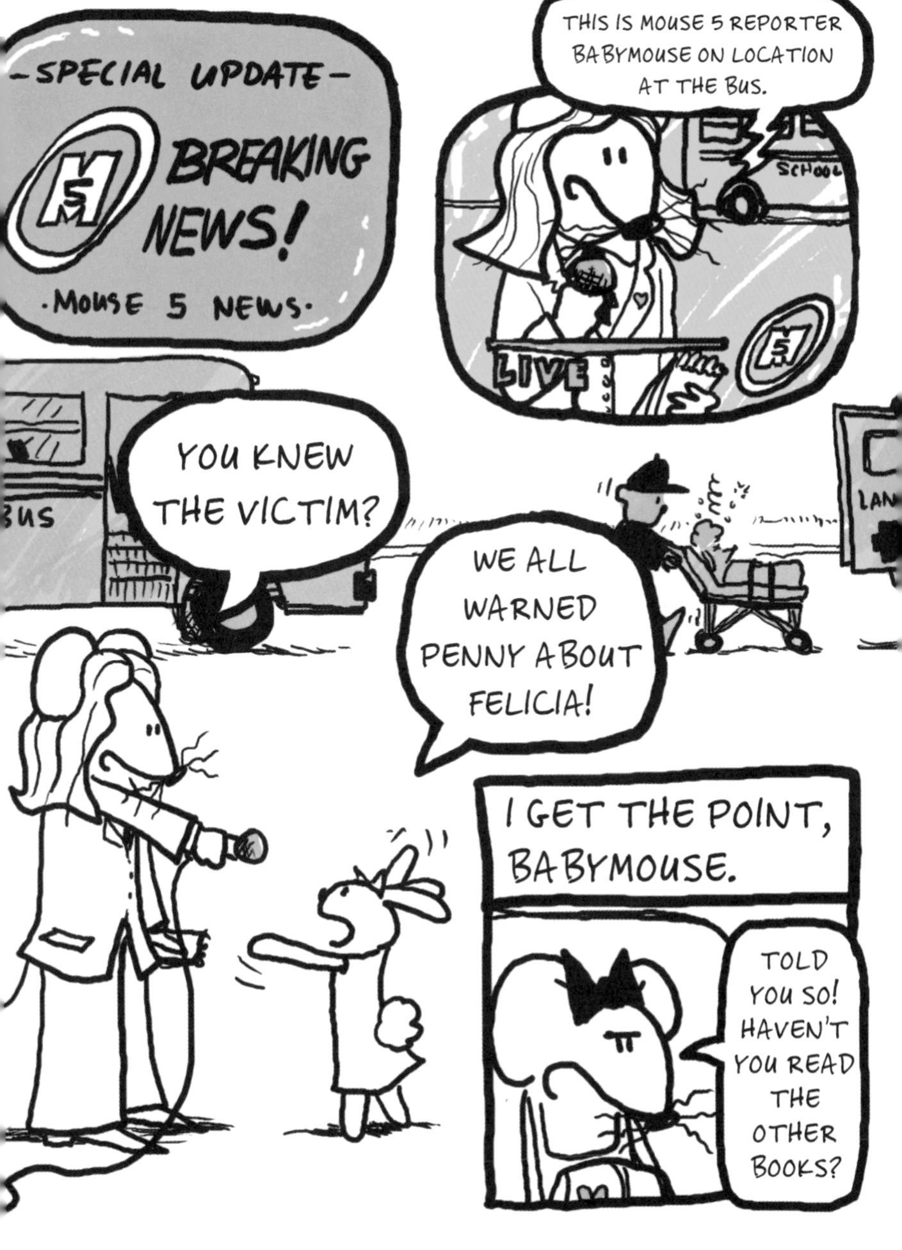

-SPECIAL UPDATE-
BREAKING NEWS!
·MOUSE 5 NEWS·
THIS IS MOUSE 5 REPORTER BABYMOUSE ON LOCATION AT THE BUS.
SCHOOL
LIVE
BUS
YOU KNEW THE VICTIM?
WE ALL WARNED PENNY ABOUT FELICIA!
I GET THE POINT, BABYMOUSE.
TOLD YOU SO! HAVEN'T YOU READ THE OTHER BOOKS?

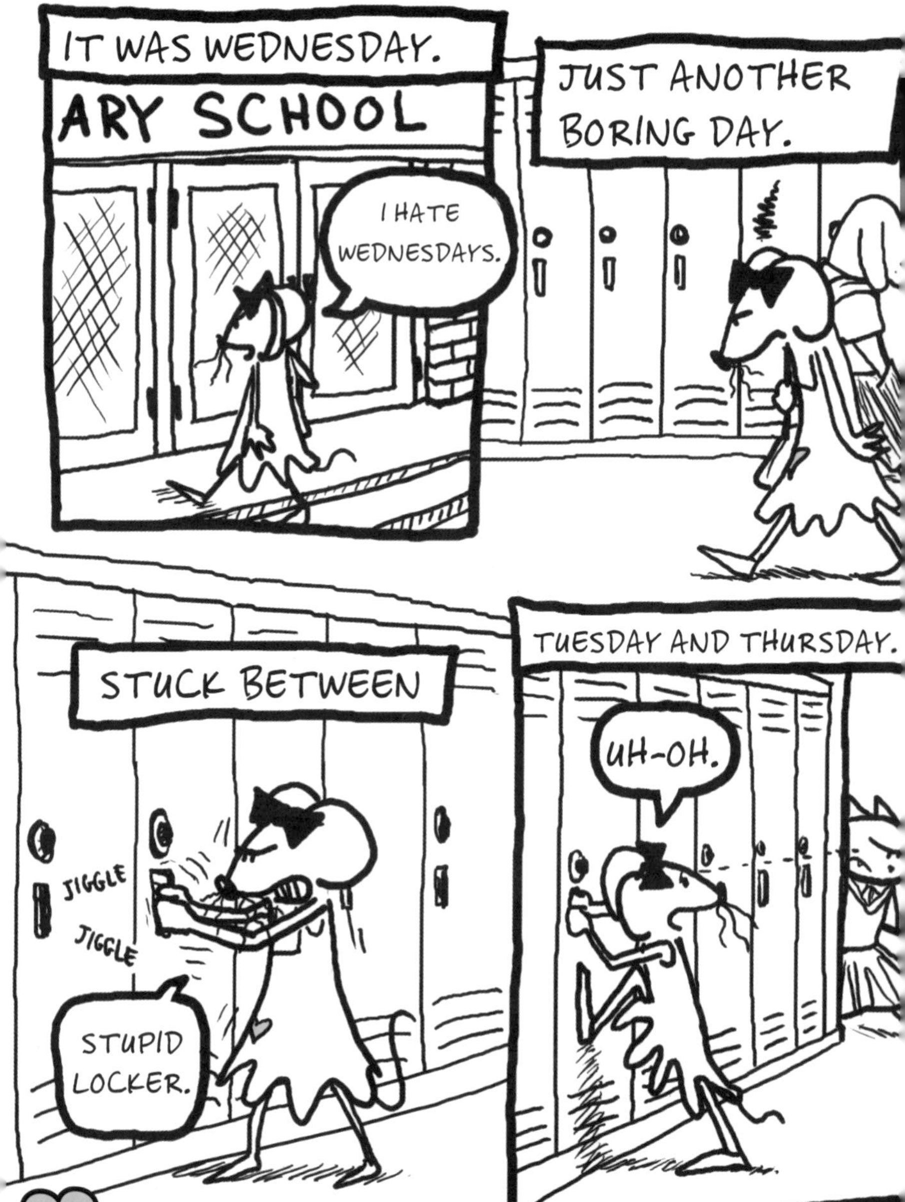

IT WAS WEDNESDAY.
ARY SCHOOL
I HATE WEDNESDAYS.
JUST ANOTHER BORING DAY.
STUCK BETWEEN
JIGGLE
JIGGLE
STUPID LOCKER.
TUESDAY AND THURSDAY.
UH-OH.

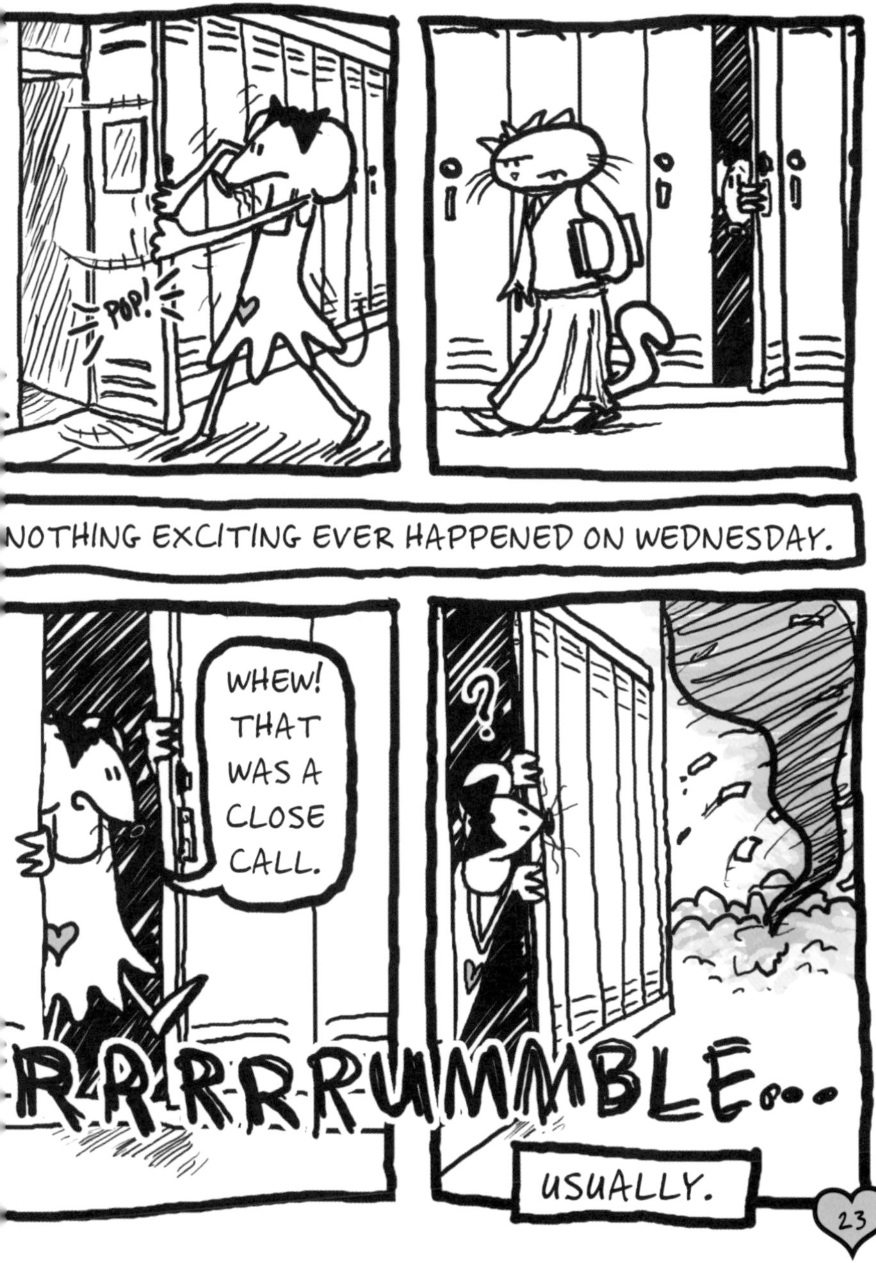
POP!
NOTHING EXCITING EVER HAPPENED ON WEDNESDAY.
WHEW! THAT WAS A CLOSE CALL.
?
RRRRRRUMMMBLE...
USUALLY.

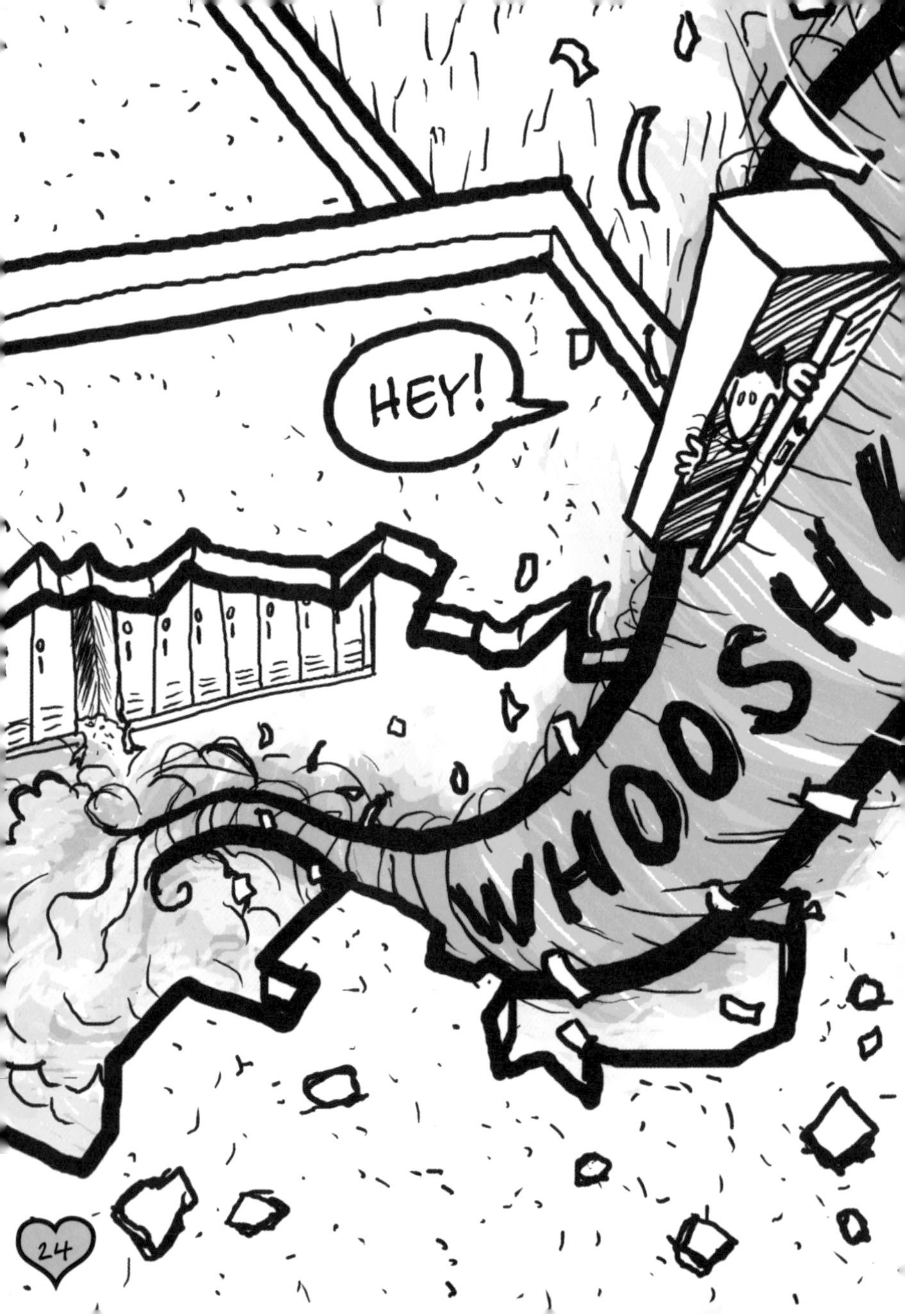
HEY!
WHOOSH

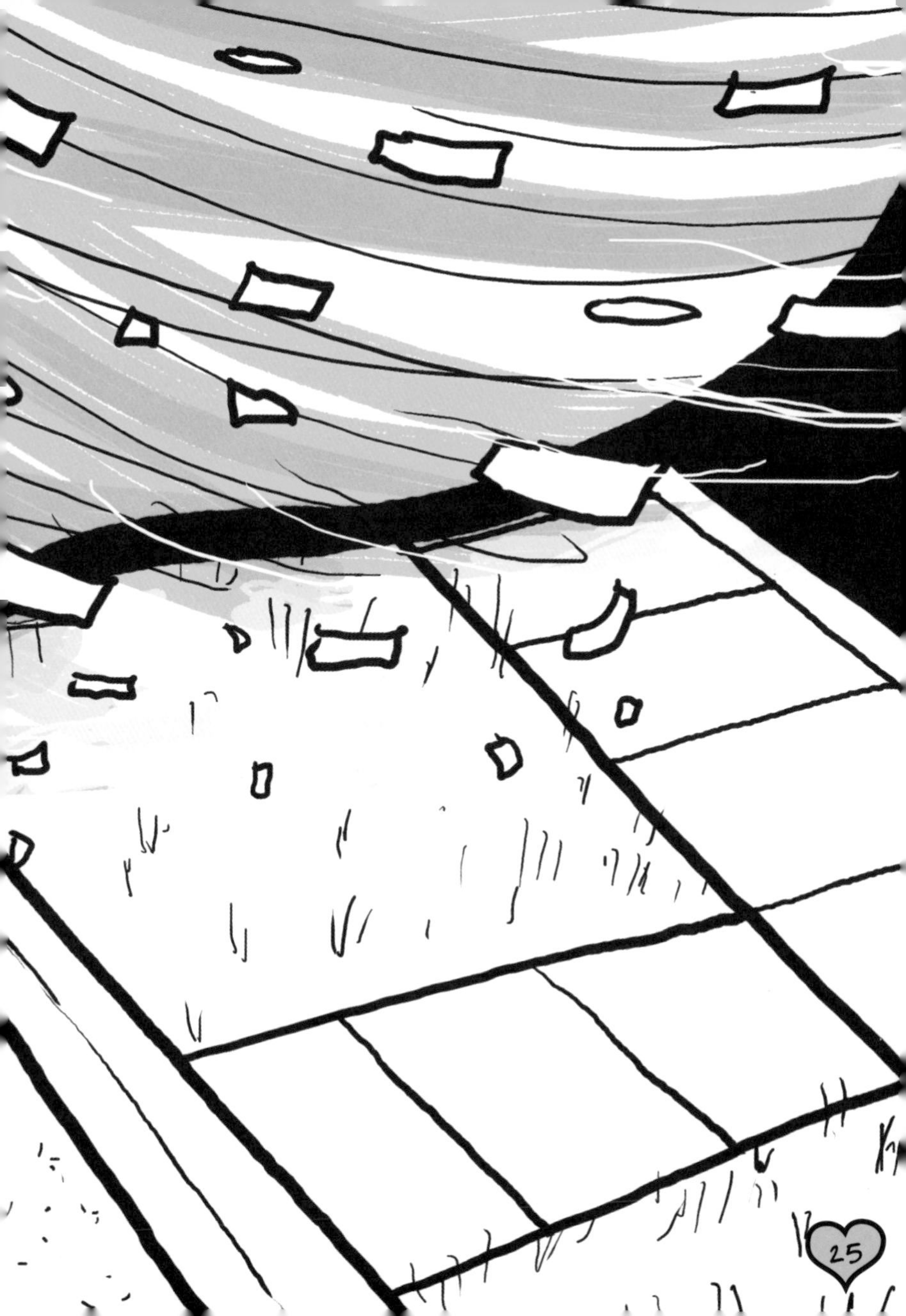

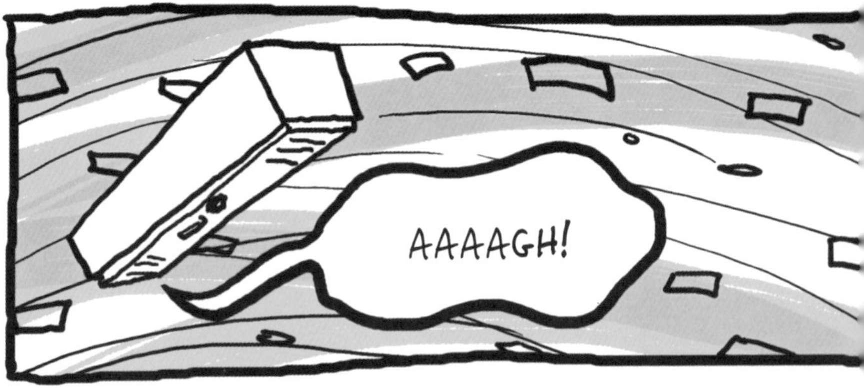
AAAAGH!

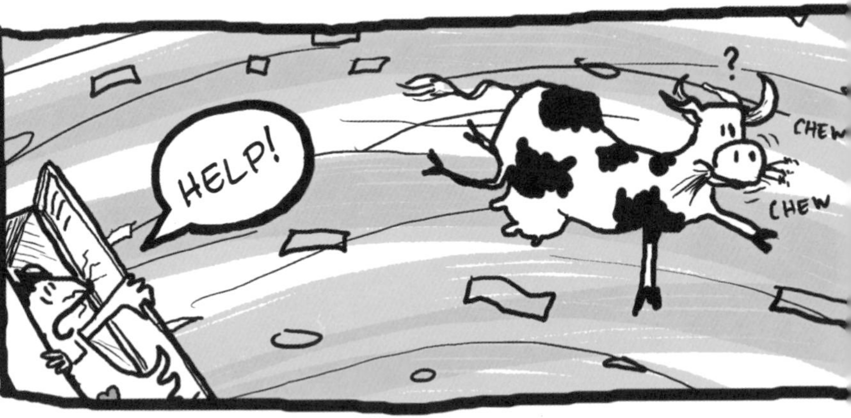
HELP!
?
CHEW
CHEW

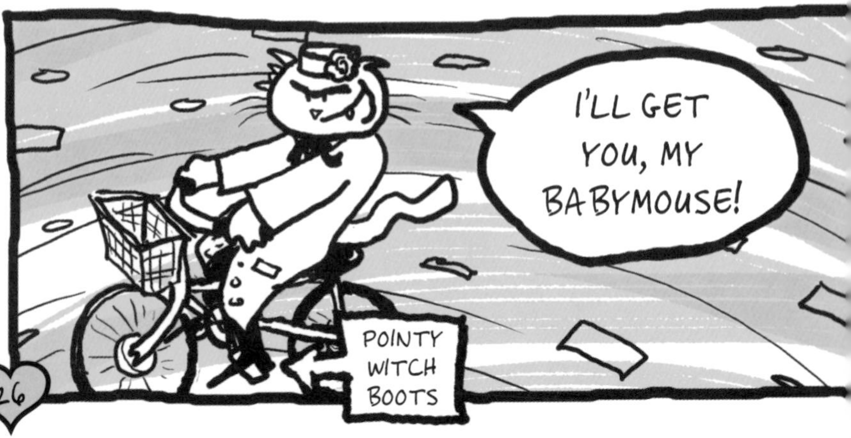
I'LL GET YOU, MY BABYMOUSE!
POINTY WITCH BOOTS

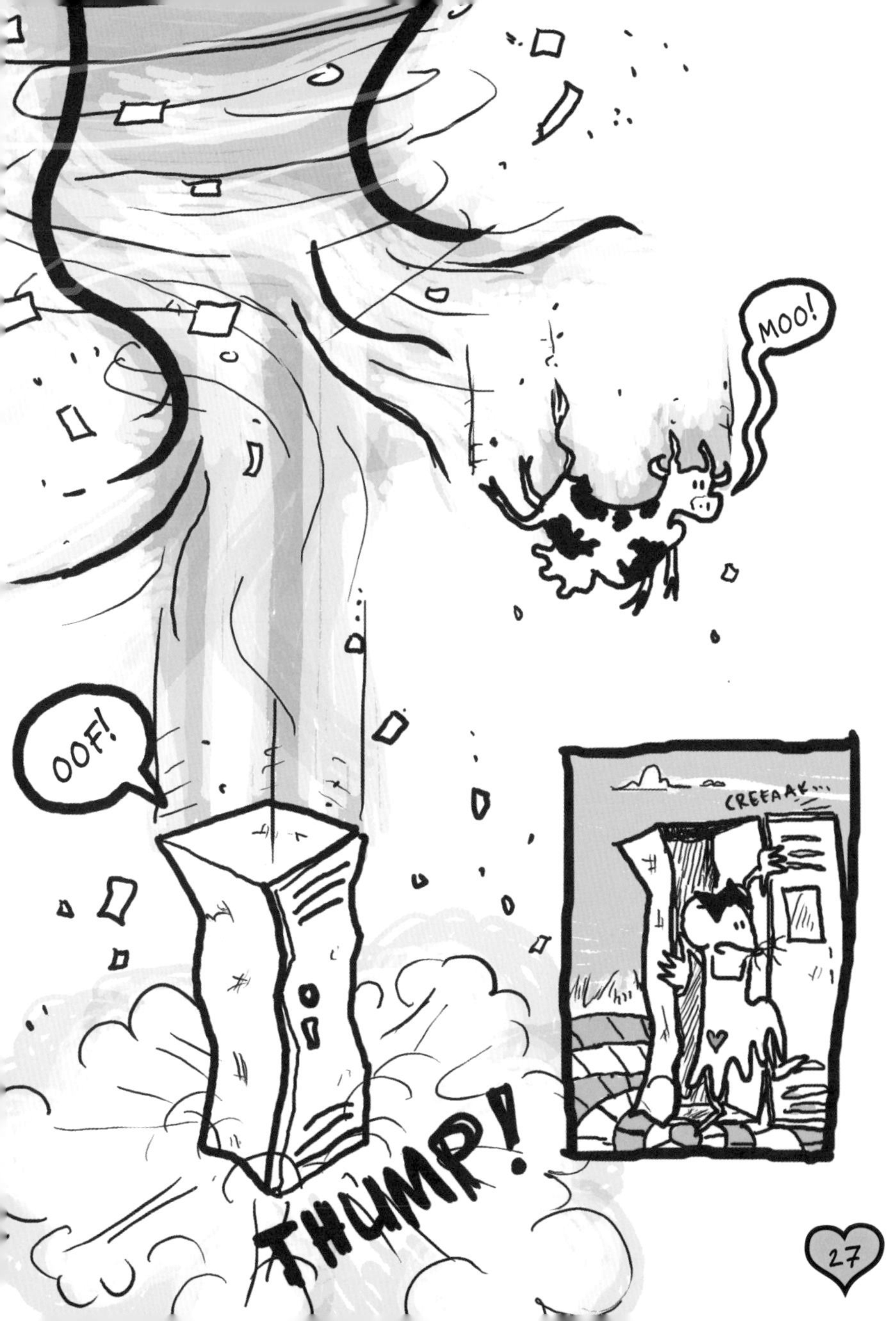
MOO!
OOF!
CREEAAK...
THUMP!

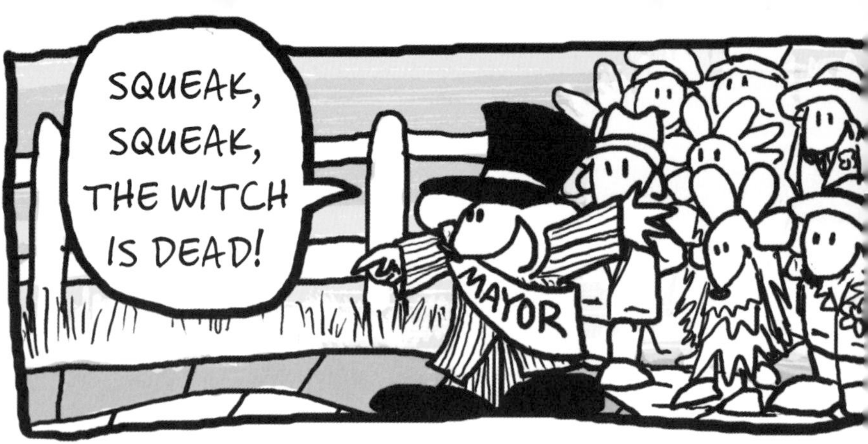
SQUEAK, SQUEAK, THE WITCH IS DEAD!
MAYOR

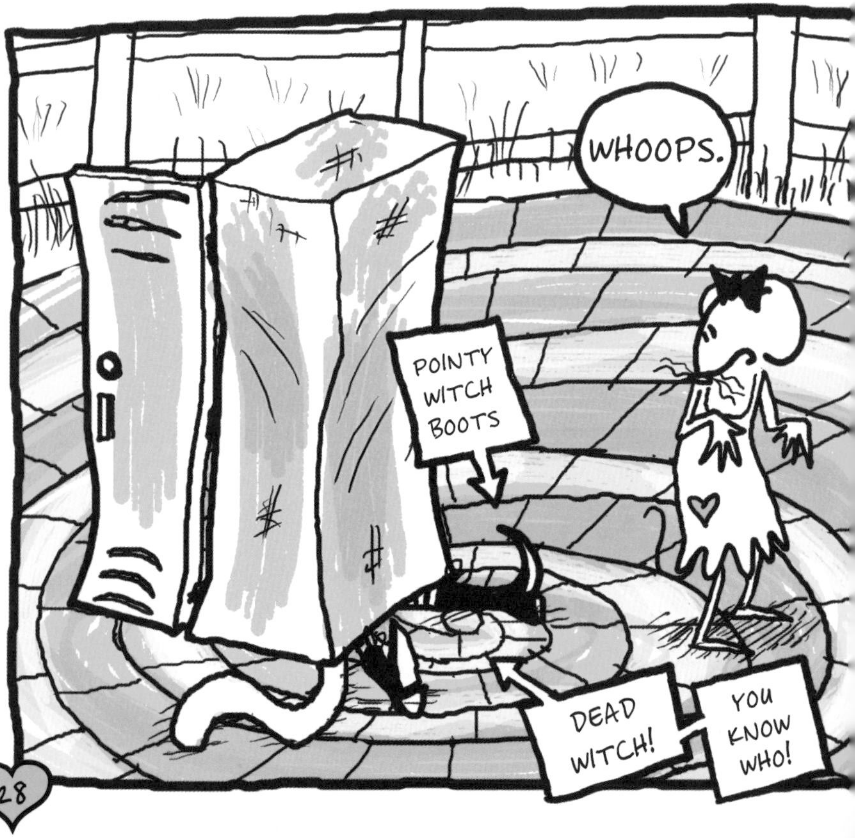
WHOOPS.
POINTY WITCH BOOTS
DEAD WITCH!
YOU KNOW WHO!

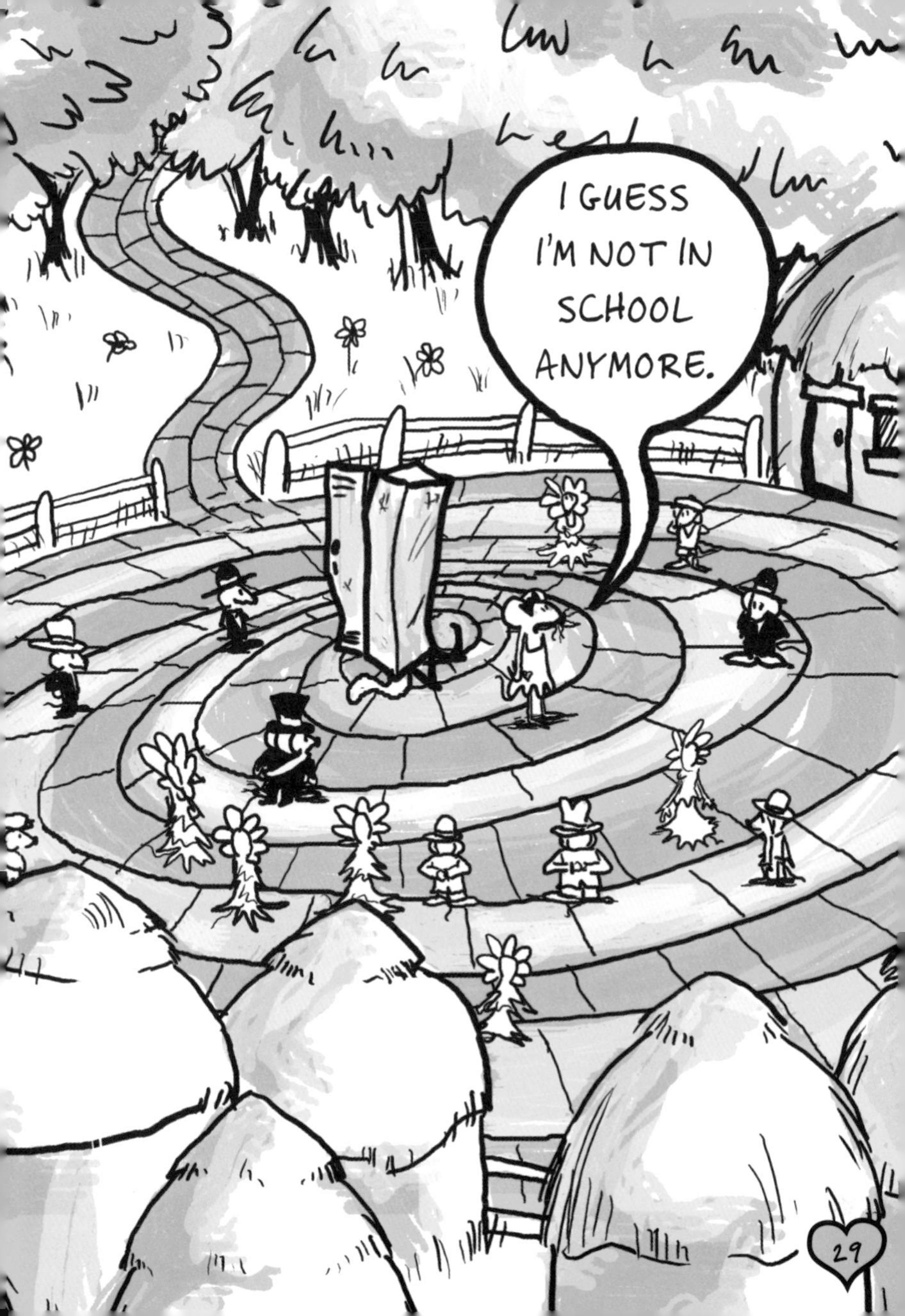
I GUESS I'M NOT IN SCHOOL ANYMORE.

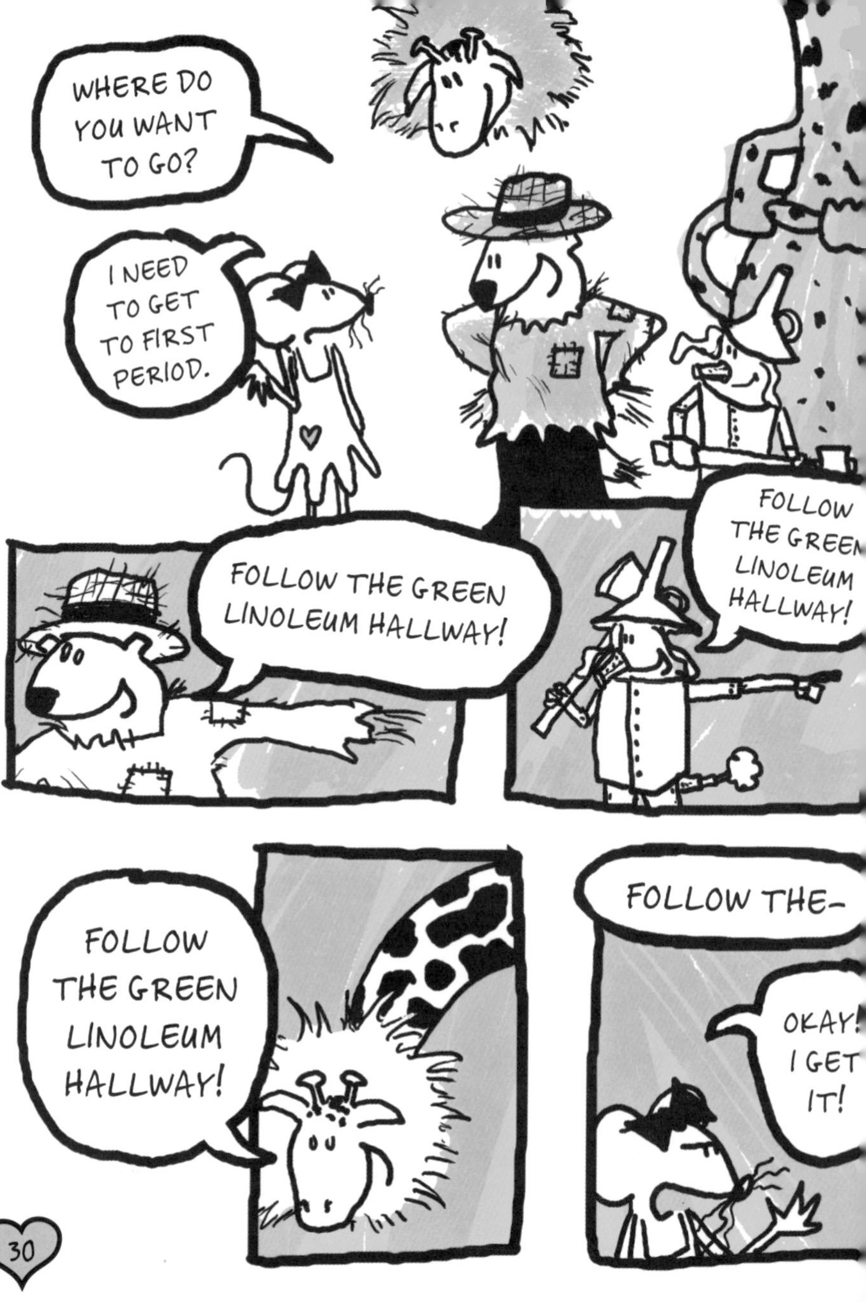
WHERE DO YOU WANT TO GO?
I NEED TO GET TO FIRST PERIOD.
FOLLOW THE GREEN LINOLEUM HALLWAY!
FOLLOW THE GREEN LINOLEUM HALLWAY!
FOLLOW THE GREEN LINOLEUM HALLWAY!
FOLLOW THE-
OKAY! I GET IT!

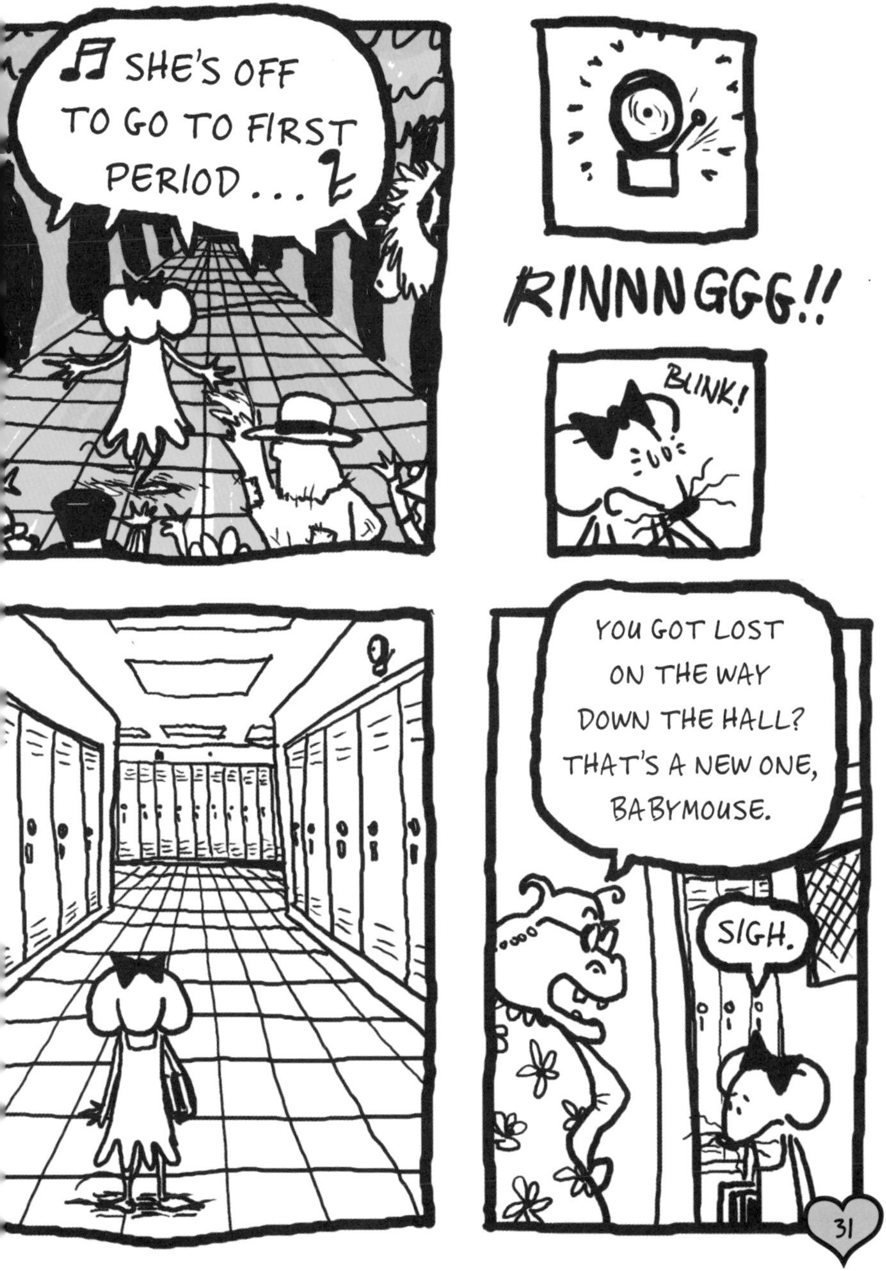
♫ SHE'S OFF TO GO TO FIRST PERIOD...
RINNNGGG!!
BLINK!
YOU GOT LOST ON THE WAY DOWN THE HALL? THAT'S A NEW ONE, BABYMOUSE.
SIGH.

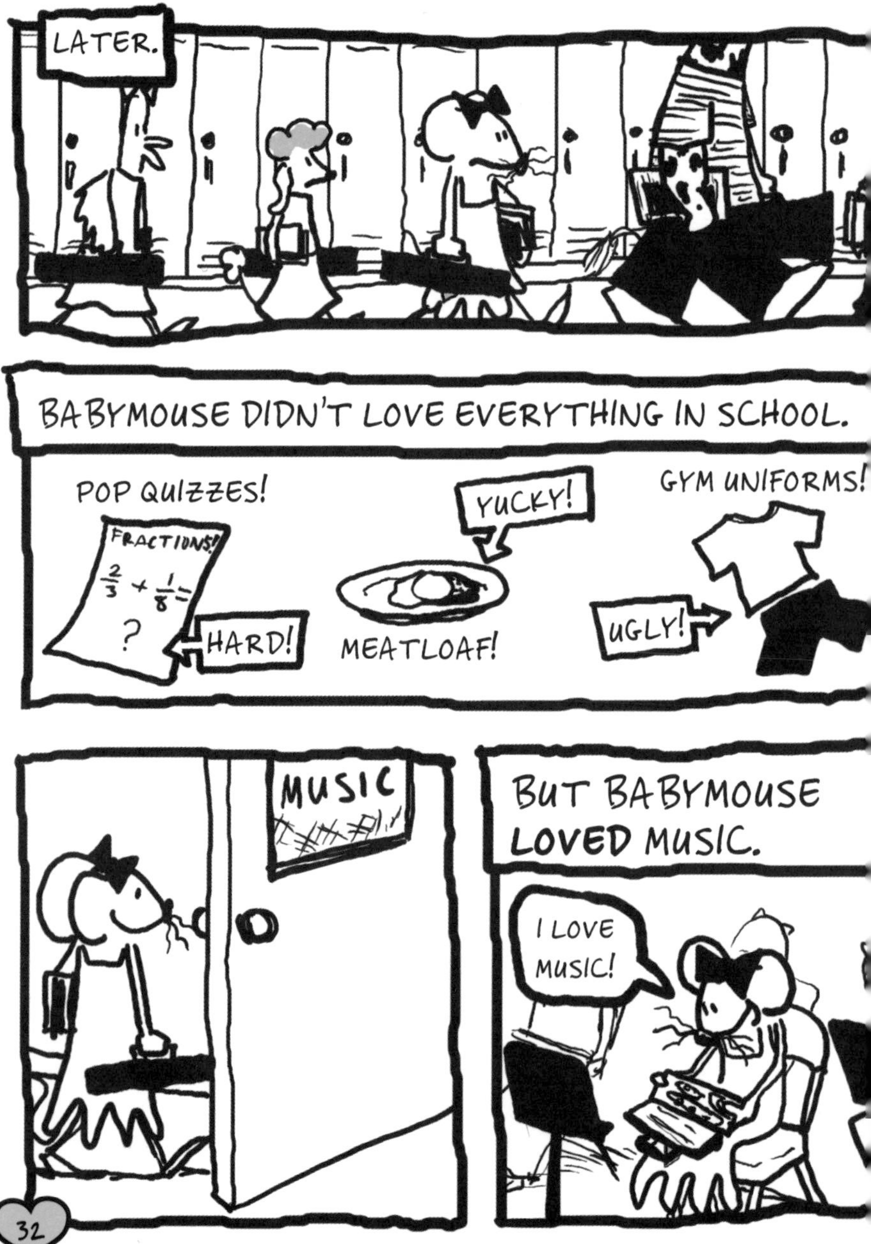
LATER.
BABYMOUSE DIDN'T LOVE EVERYTHING IN SCHOOL.
POP QUIZZES!
FRACTIONS!
HARD!
YUCKY!
MEATLOAF!
GYM UNIFORMS!
UGLY!
MUSIC
BUT BABYMOUSE LOVED MUSIC.
I LOVE MUSIC!

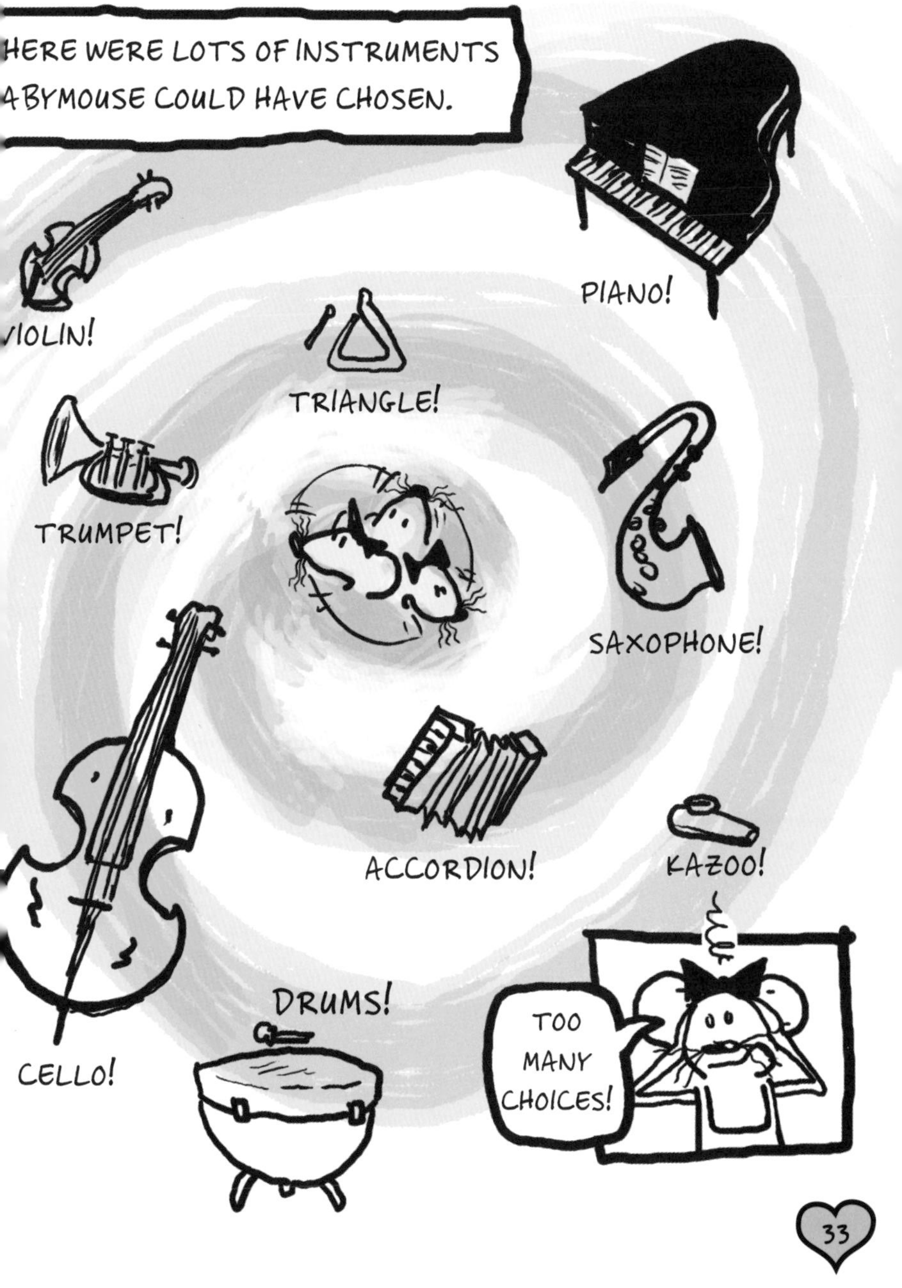
HERE WERE LOTS OF INSTRUMENTS
ABYMOUSE COULD HAVE CHOSEN.
IOLIN!
PIANO!
TRIANGLE!
TRUMPET!
SAXOPHONE!
ACCORDION!
KAZOO!
DRUMS!
CELLO!
TOO MANY CHOICES!

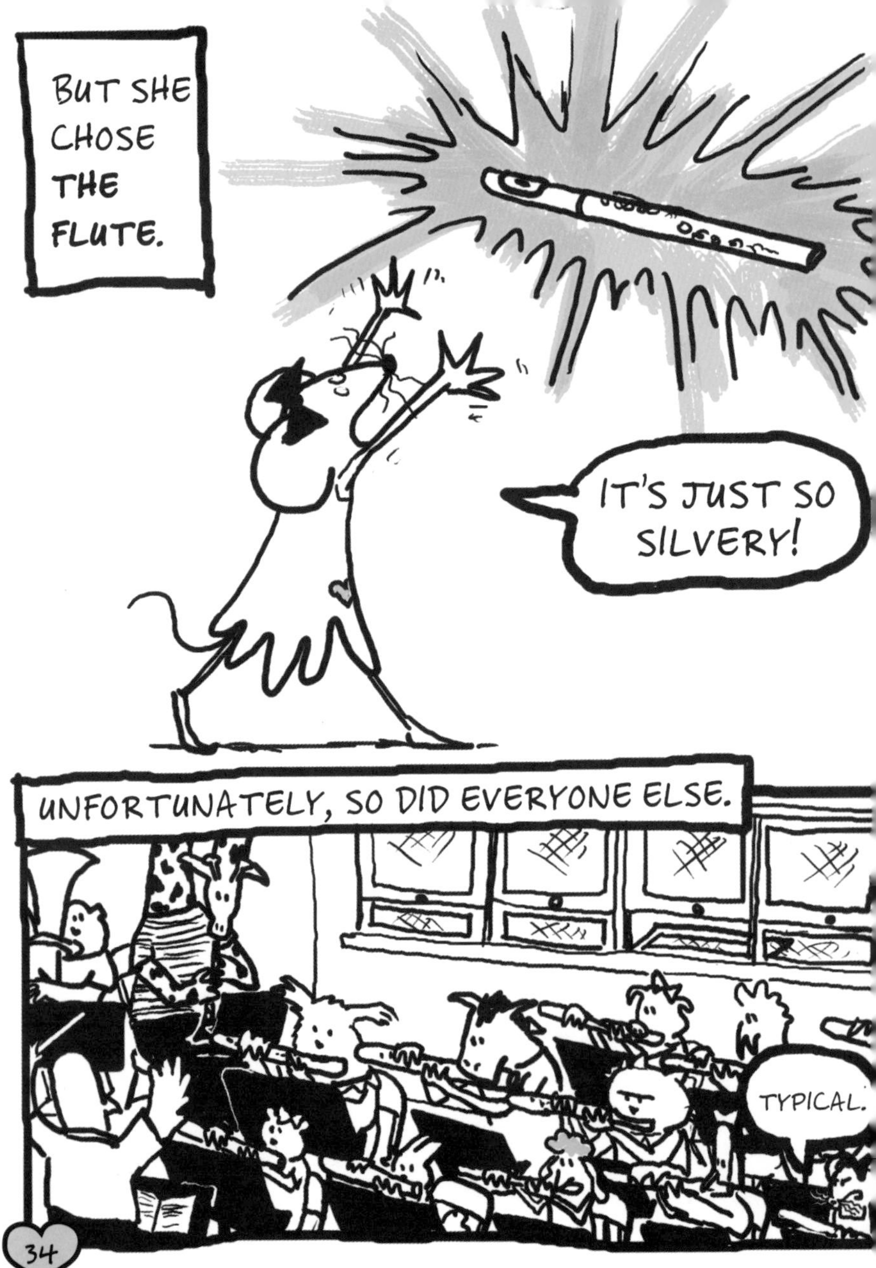
BUT SHE CHOSE THE FLUTE.
IT'S JUST SO SILVERY!
UNFORTUNATELY, SO DID EVERYONE ELSE.
TYPICAL.

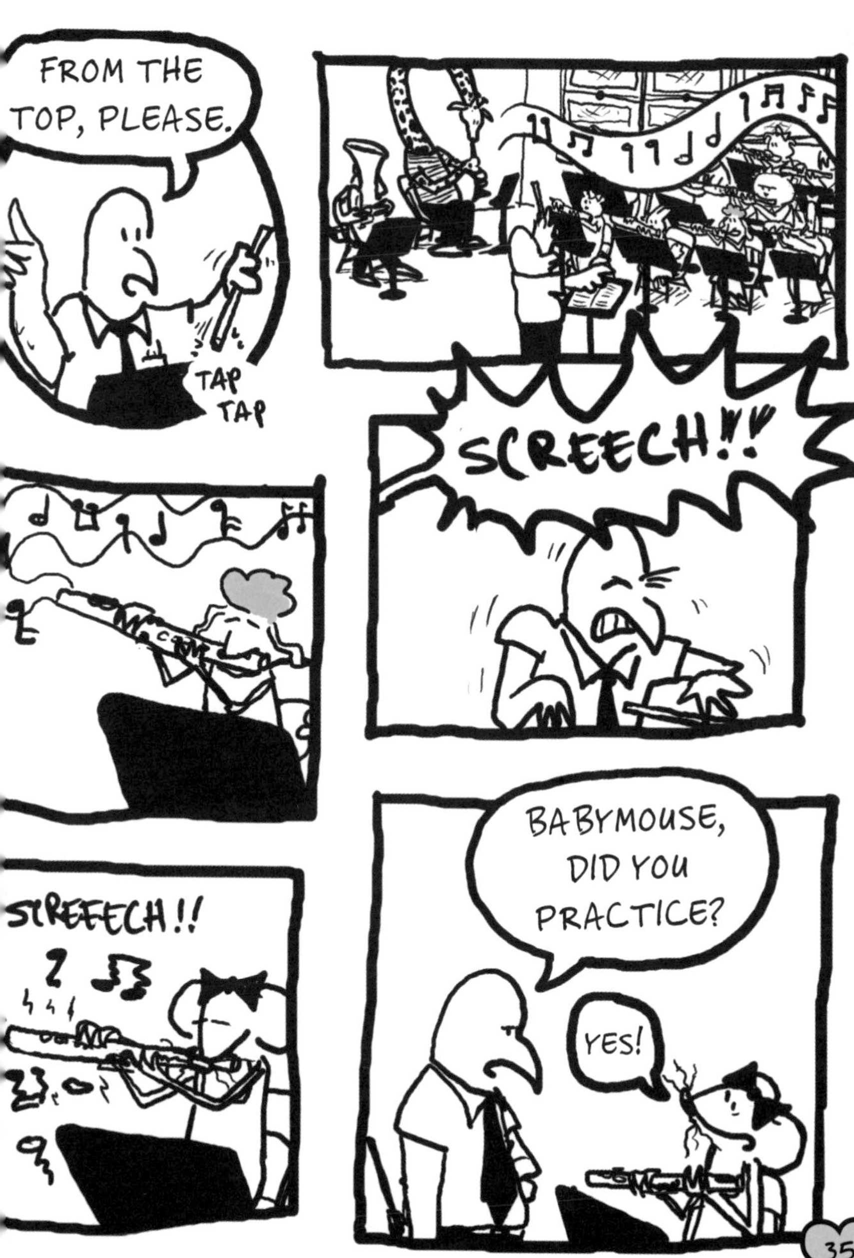
FROM THE TOP, PLEASE.
TAP TAP
SCREECH!!!
SCREEECH!!
BABYMOUSE, DID YOU PRACTICE?
YES!

THE NIGHT BEFORE.

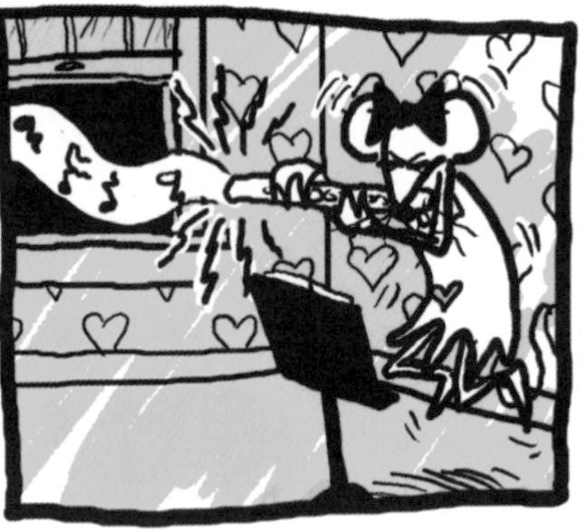

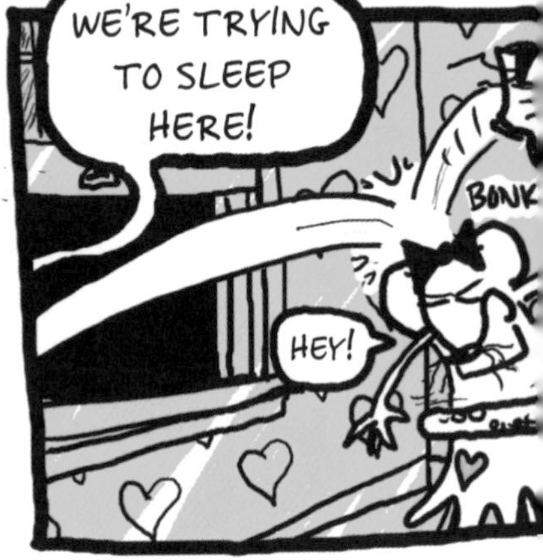
WE'RE TRYING TO SLEEP HERE!
BONK
HEY!

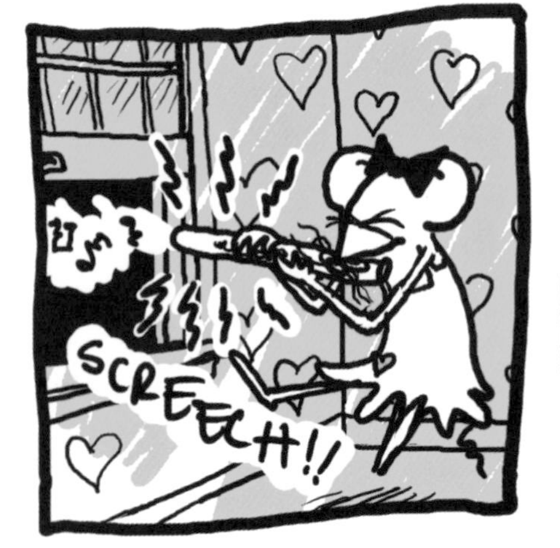
SCREEECH!!

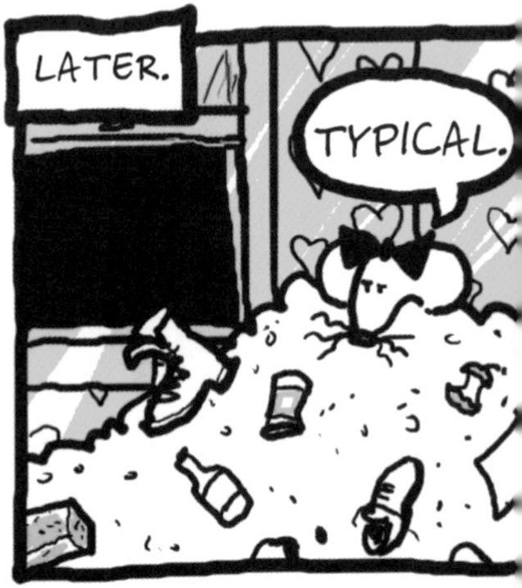
LATER.
TYPICAL.

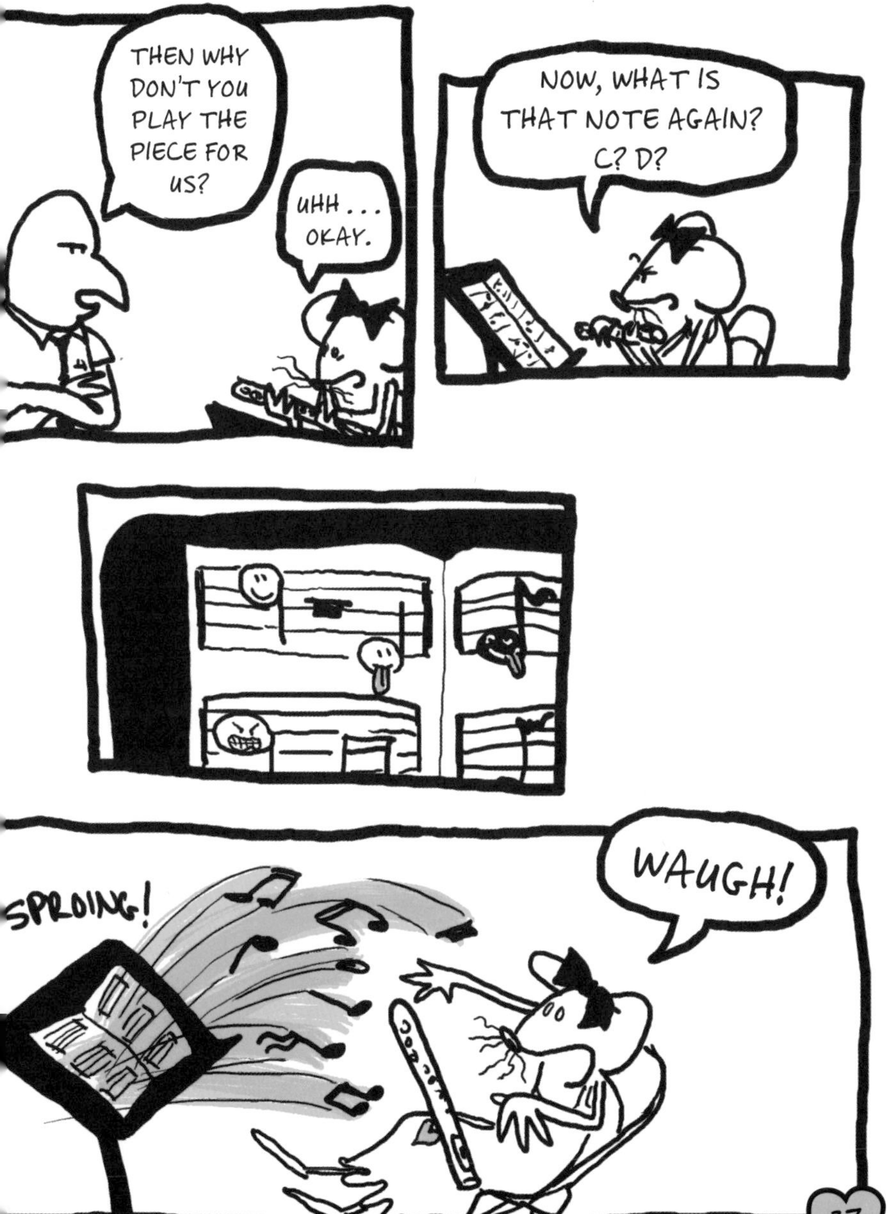
THEN WHY DON'T YOU PLAY THE PIECE FOR US?
UHH . . . OKAY.
NOW, WHAT IS THAT NOTE AGAIN? C? D?
SPROING!
WAUGH!

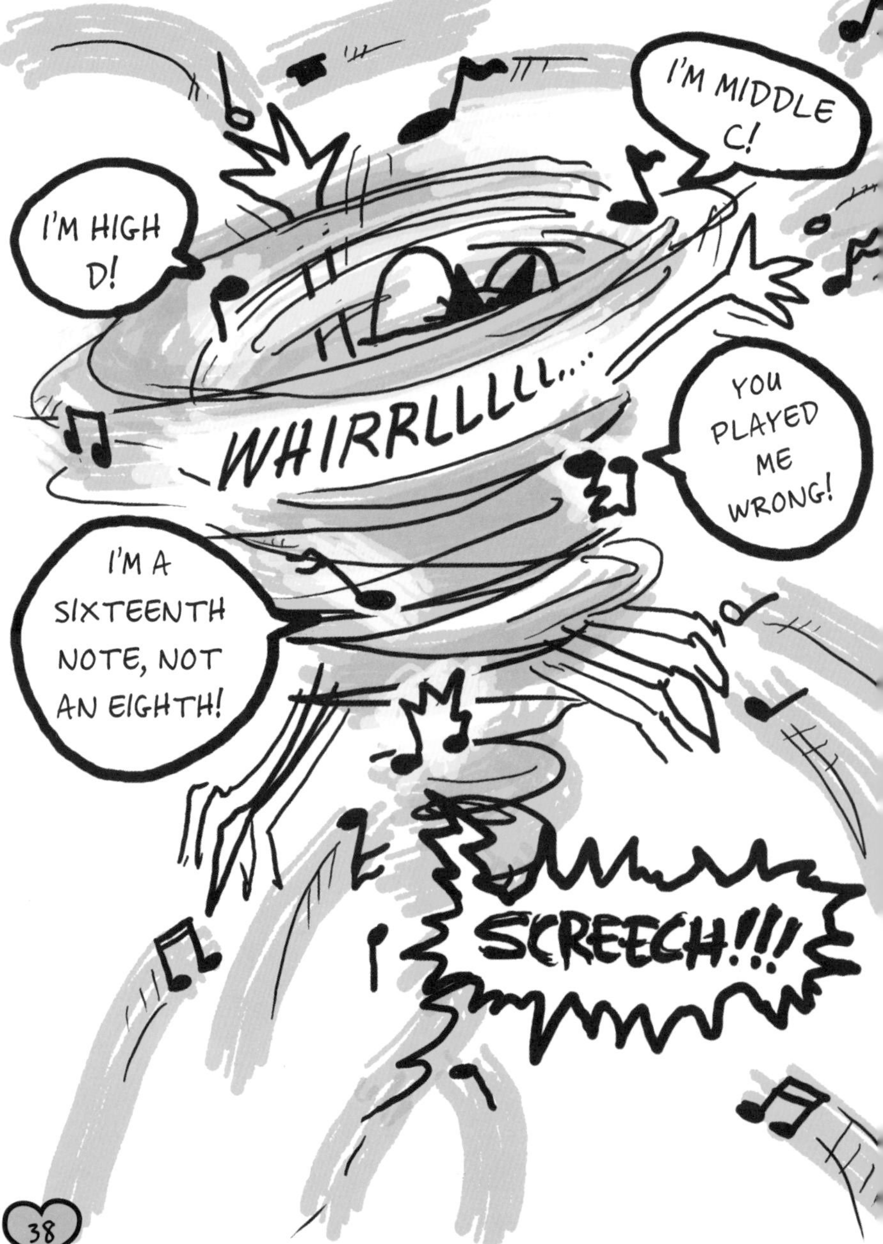
I'M MIDDLE C!
I'M HIGH D!
WHIRRLLLLL...
YOU PLAYED ME WRONG!
I'M A SIXTEENTH NOTE, NOT AN EIGHTH!
SCREECH!!!

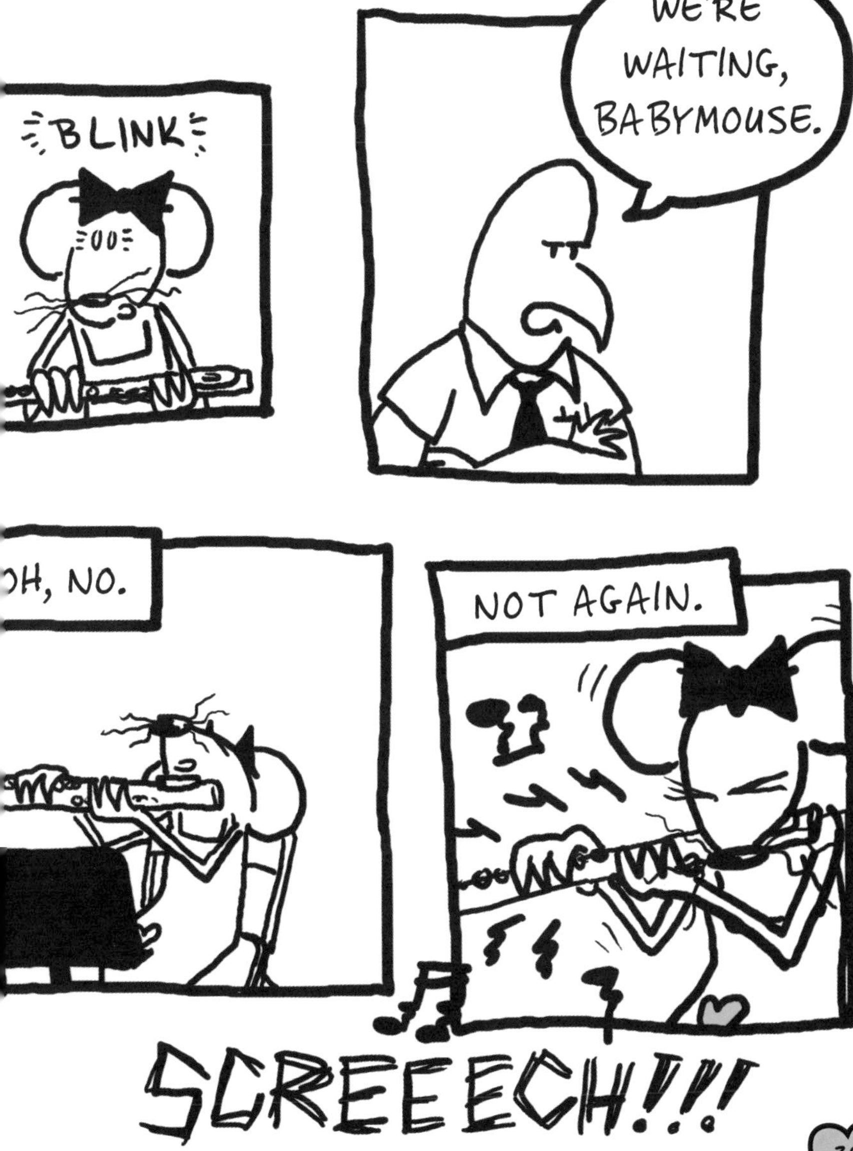
BLINK
WE'RE WAITING, BABYMOUSE.
OH, NO.
NOT AGAIN.
SCREEECH!!!!

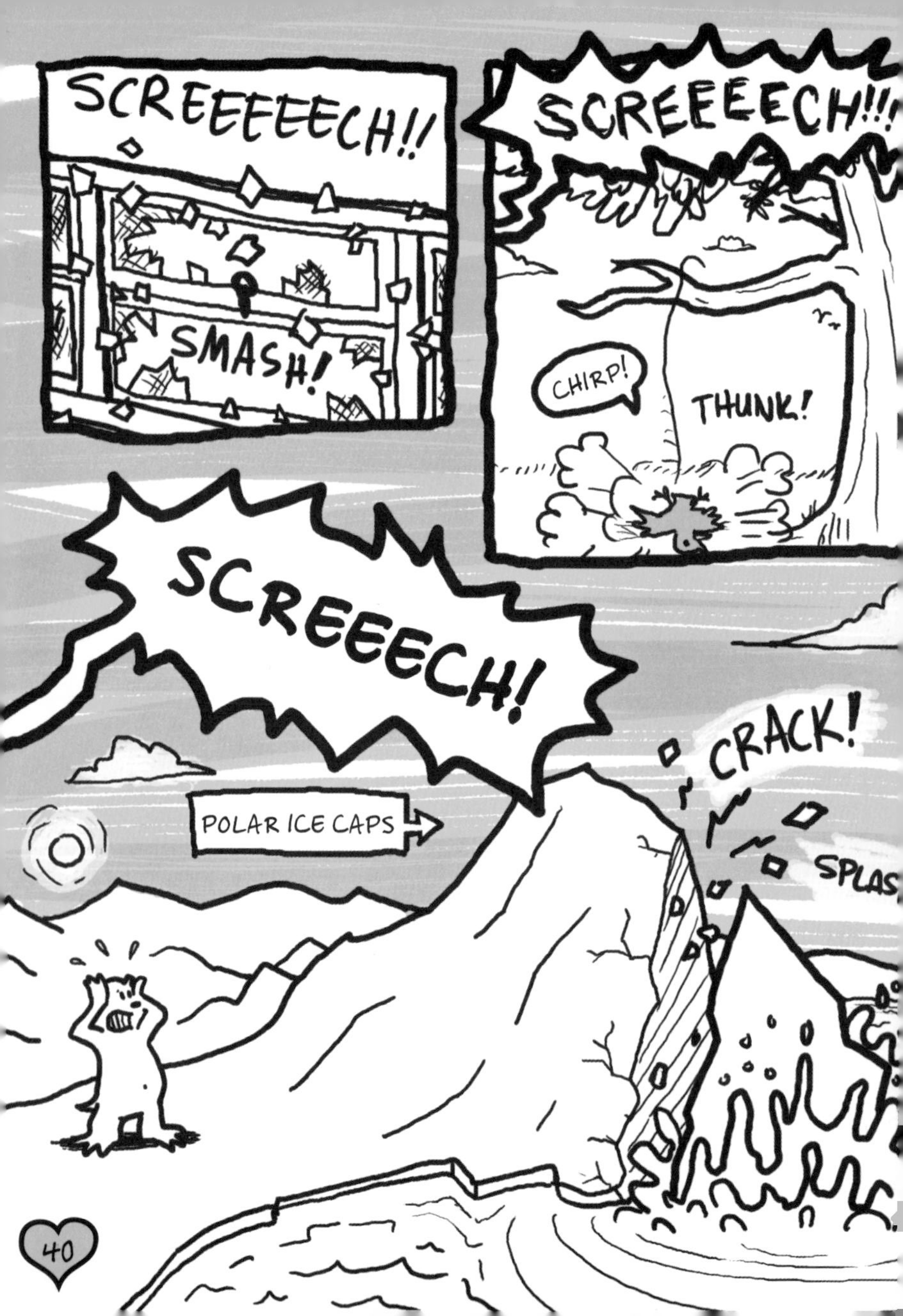
SCREEEEEECH!!
SMASH!
SCREEEEECH!!!
CHIRP!
THUNK!
SCREEEECH!
POLAR ICE CAPS
CRACK!
SPLAS

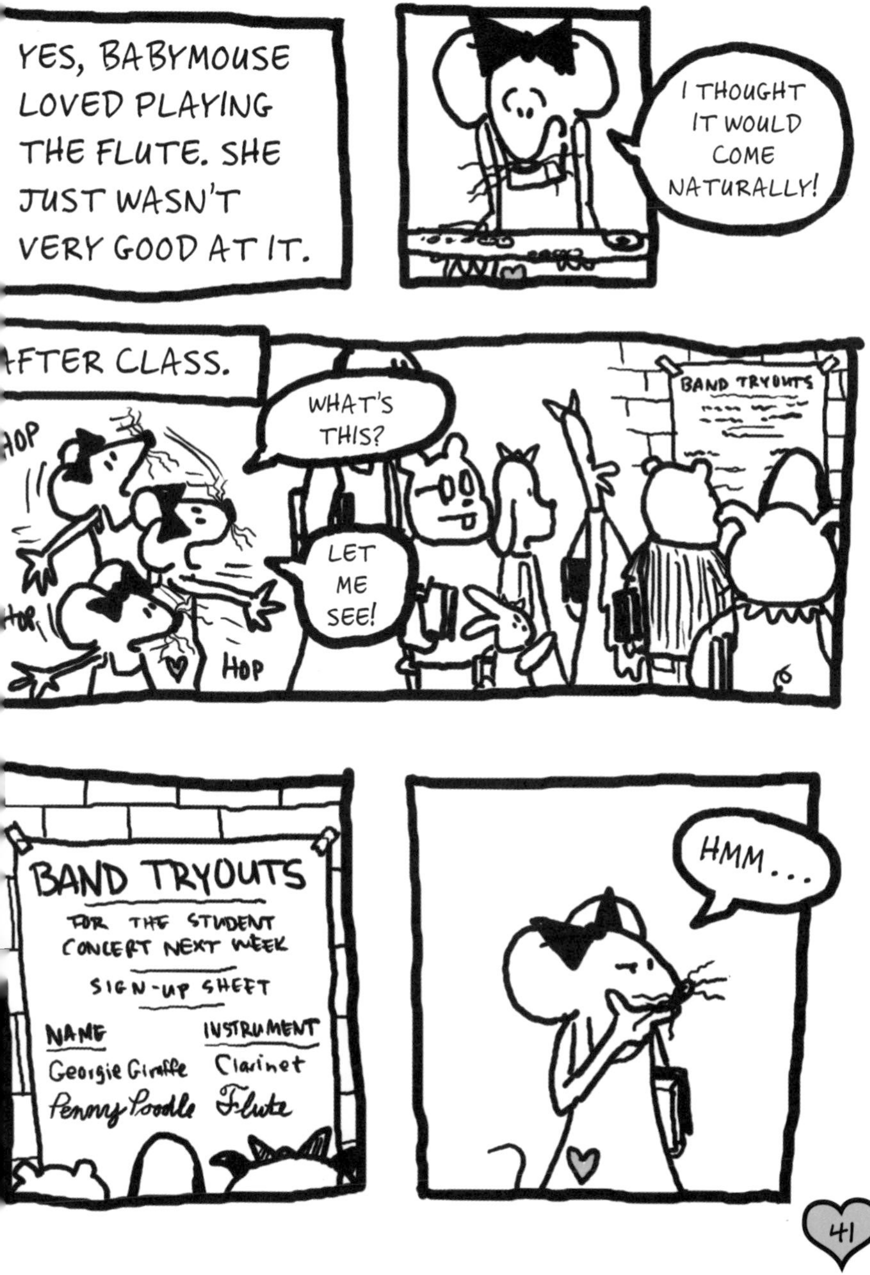

YES, BABYMOUSE LOVED PLAYING THE FLUTE. SHE JUST WASN'T VERY GOOD AT IT.
I THOUGHT IT WOULD COME NATURALLY!
AFTER CLASS.
BAND TRYOUTS
WHAT'S THIS?
HOP
HOP
HOP
LET ME SEE!
BAND TRYOUTS
FOR THE STUDENT CONCERT NEXT WEEK
SIGN-UP SHEET
NAME INSTRUMENT
Georgie Giraffe Clarinet
Penny Poodle Flute
HMM...

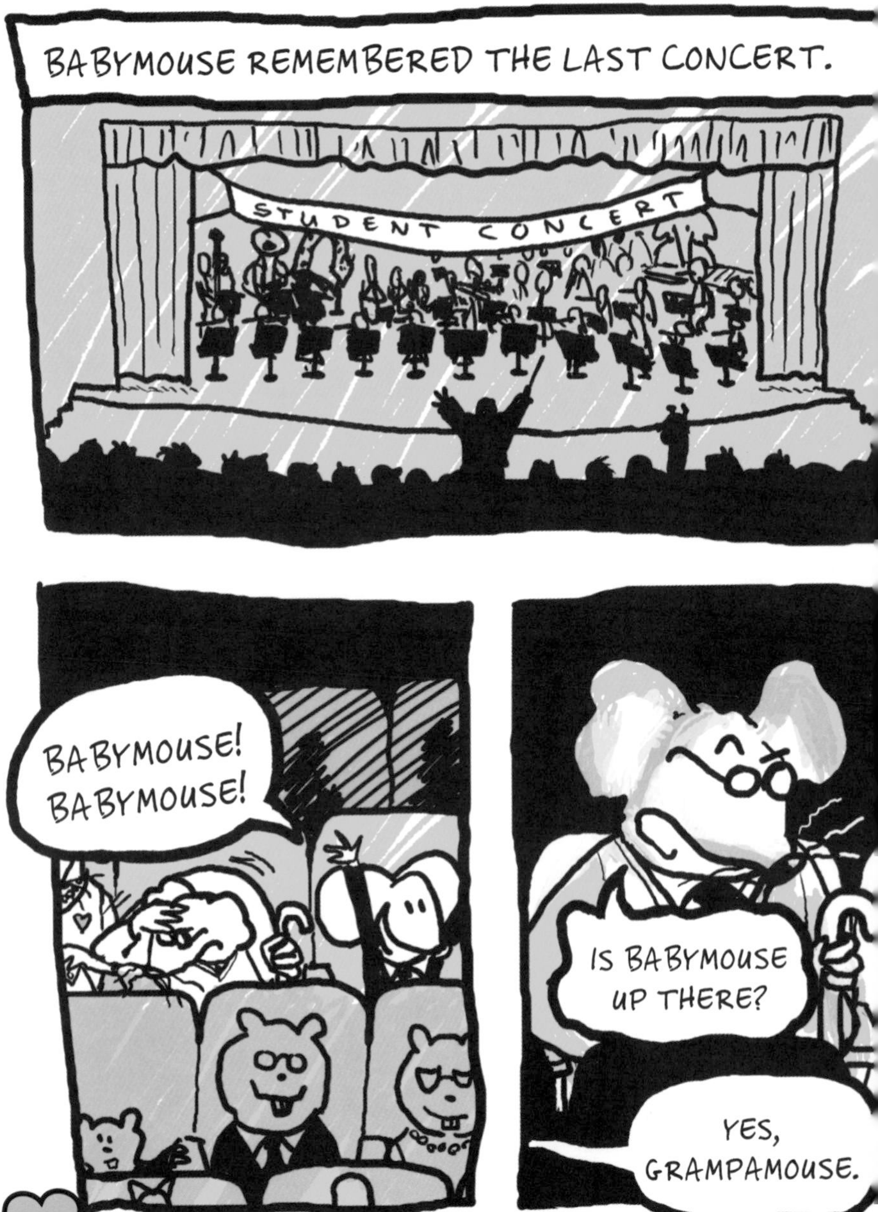
BABYMOUSE REMEMBERED THE LAST CONCERT.
STUDENT CONCERT
BABYMOUSE! BABYMOUSE!
IS BABYMOUSE UP THERE?
YES, GRAMPAMOUSE.

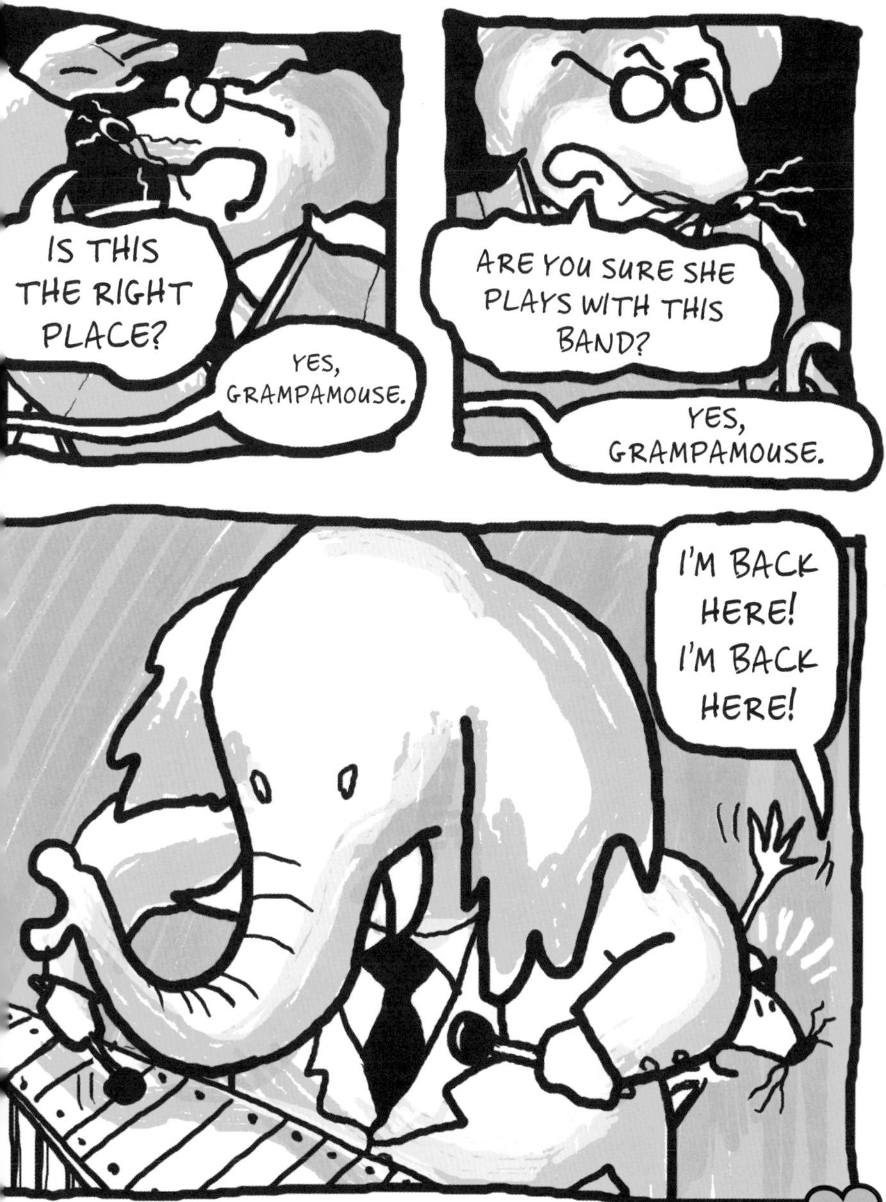
IS THIS THE RIGHT PLACE?
YES, GRAMPAMOUSE.
ARE YOU SURE SHE PLAYS WITH THIS BAND?
YES, GRAMPAMOUSE.
I'M BACK HERE! I'M BACK HERE!

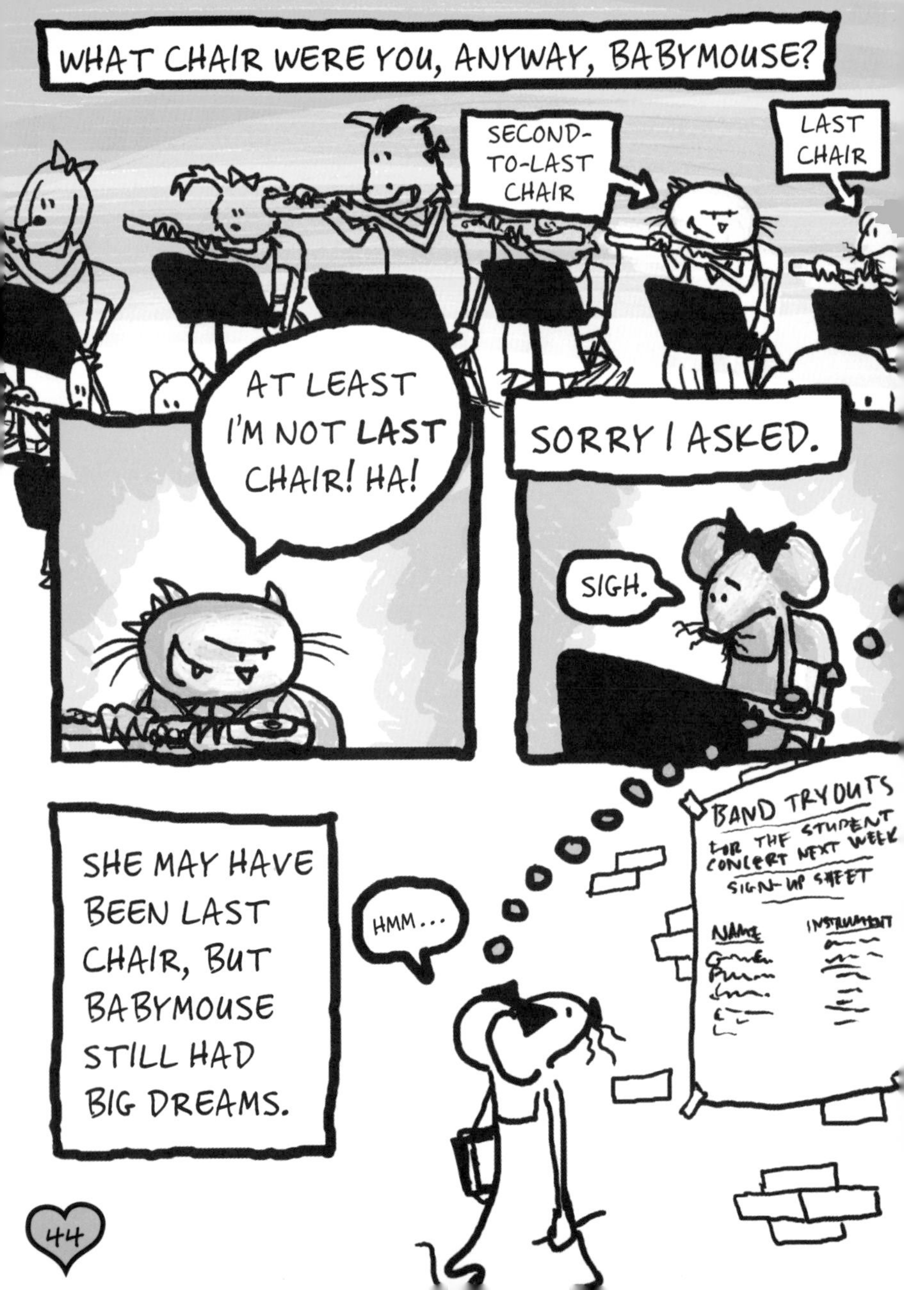
WHAT CHAIR WERE YOU, ANYWAY, BABYMOUSE?
SECOND-TO-LAST CHAIR
LAST CHAIR
AT LEAST I'M NOT **LAST** CHAIR! HA!
SORRY I ASKED.
SIGH.
SHE MAY HAVE BEEN LAST CHAIR, BUT BABYMOUSE STILL HAD BIG DREAMS.
HMM...
BAND TRYOUTS
FOR THE STUDENT CONCERT NEXT WEEK
SIGN-UP SHEET
NAME
INSTRUMENT

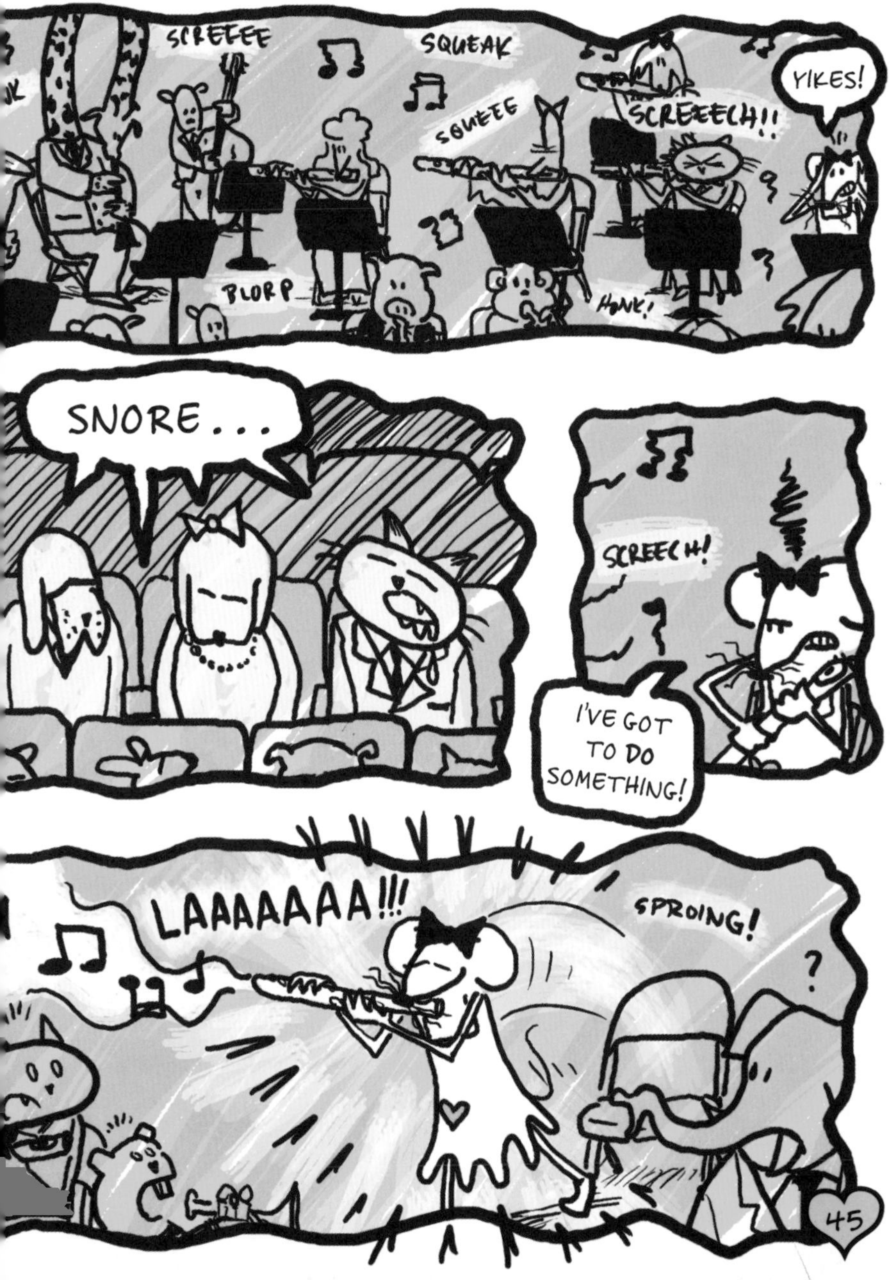
SCREEEE
SQUEAK
SQUEEE
SCREEECH!!
YIKES!
BLORP
HONK!
SNORE...
SCREECH!
I'VE GOT TO DO SOMETHING!
LAAAAAAA!!!
SPROING!
?

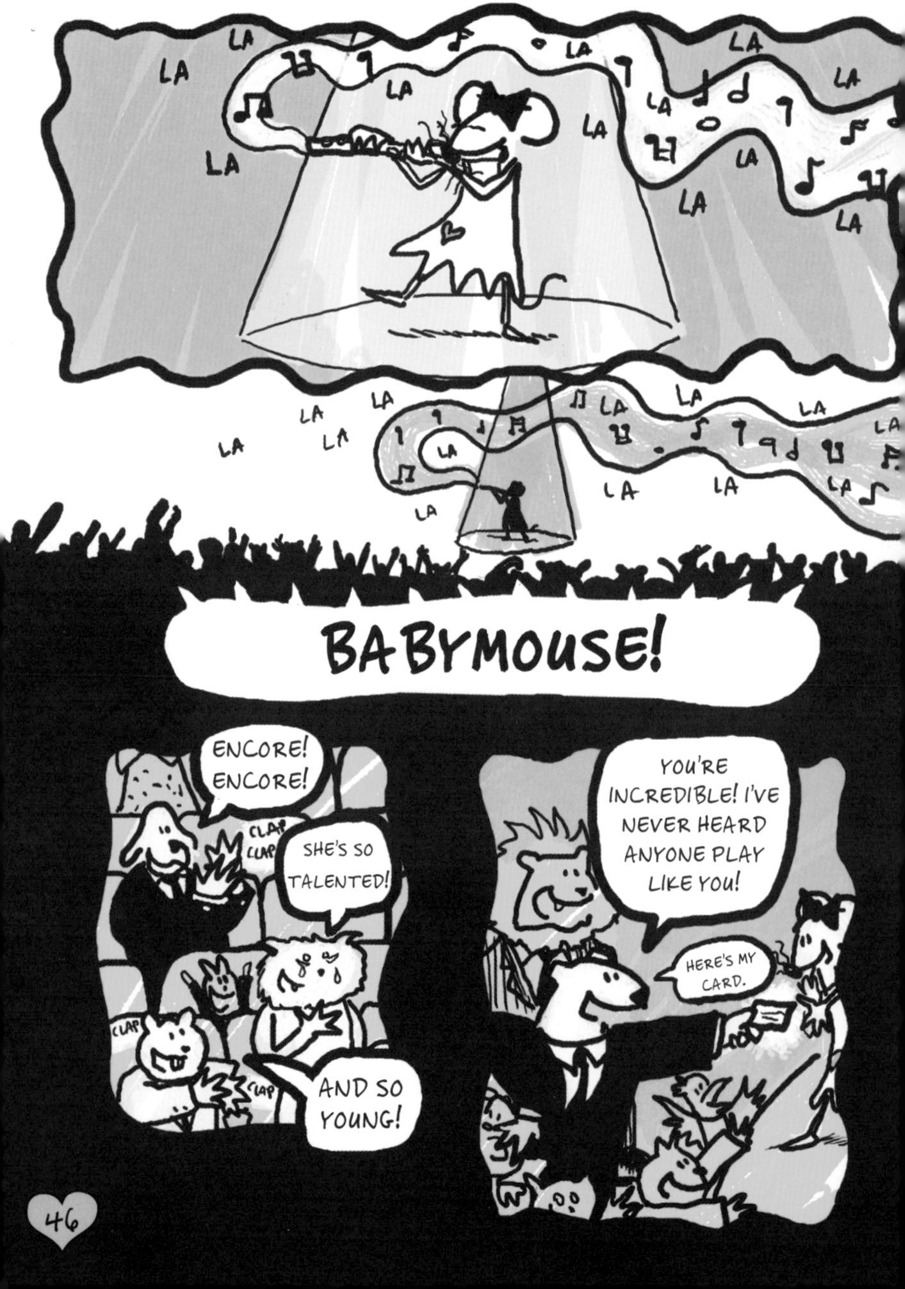
LA LA LA LA LA LA LA LA LA LA LA
BABYMOUSE!
ENCORE! ENCORE!
CLAP CLAP
SHE'S SO TALENTED!
CLAP
CLAP
AND SO YOUNG!
YOU'RE INCREDIBLE! I'VE NEVER HEARD ANYONE PLAY LIKE YOU!
HERE'S MY CARD.

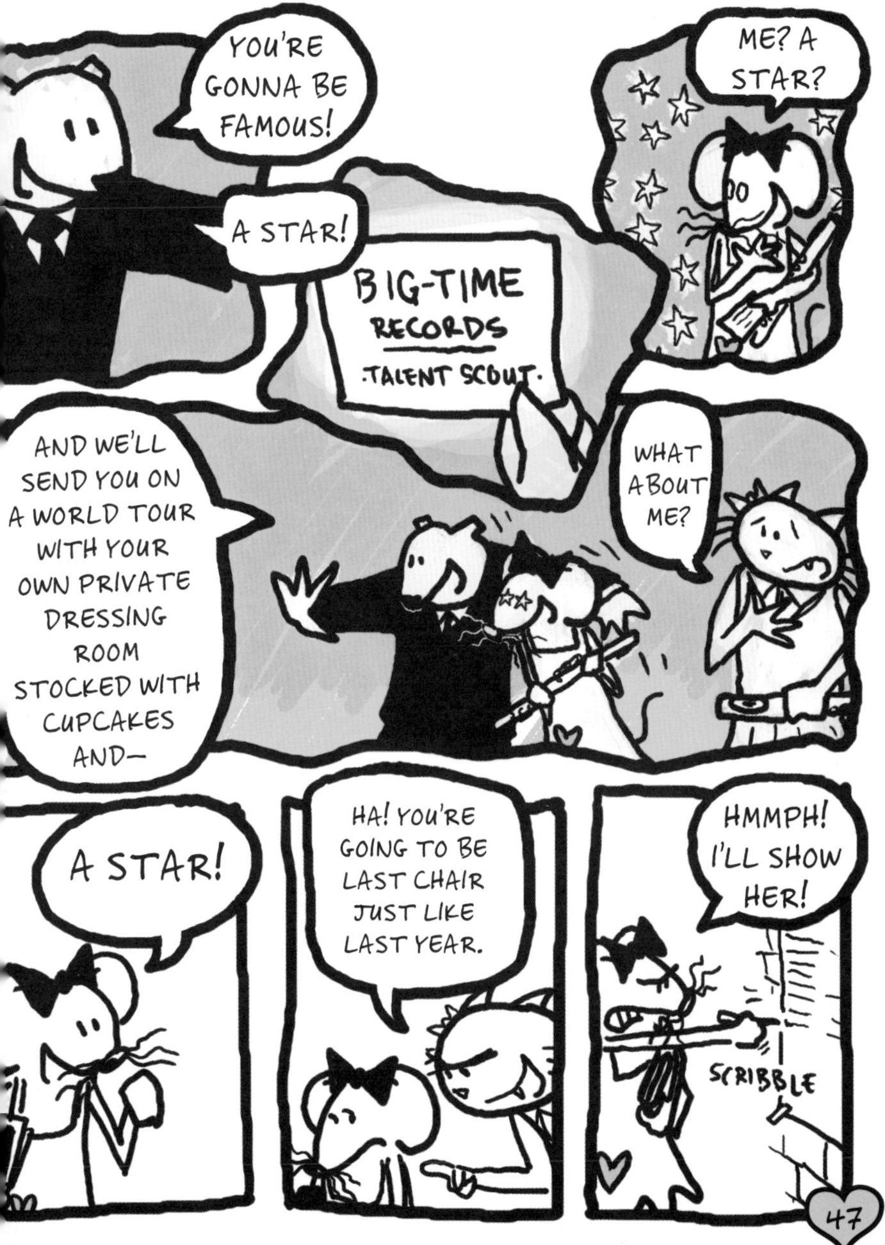
YOU'RE GONNA BE FAMOUS!
A STAR!
BIG-TIME RECORDS
·TALENT SCOUT·
ME? A STAR?
AND WE'LL SEND YOU ON A WORLD TOUR WITH YOUR OWN PRIVATE DRESSING ROOM STOCKED WITH CUPCAKES AND—
WHAT ABOUT ME?
A STAR!
HA! YOU'RE GOING TO BE LAST CHAIR JUST LIKE LAST YEAR.
HMMPH! I'LL SHOW HER!
SCRIBBLE

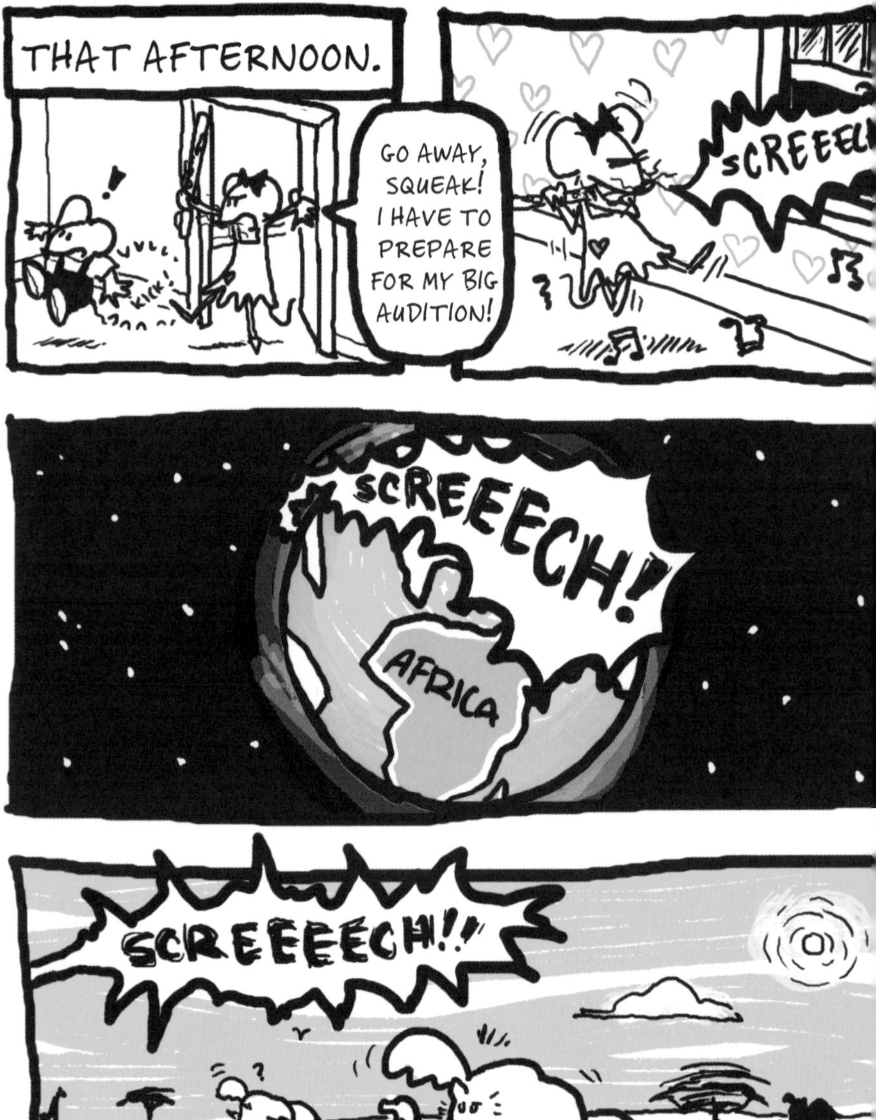
THAT AFTERNOON.
KICK!
GO AWAY, SQUEAK! I HAVE TO PREPARE FOR MY BIG AUDITION!
SCREEECH
SCREEEECH!
AFRICA
SCREEEEECH!!

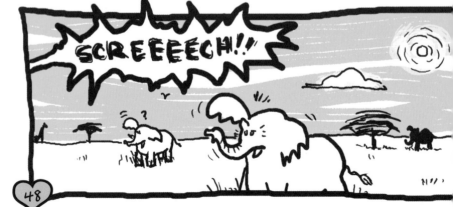

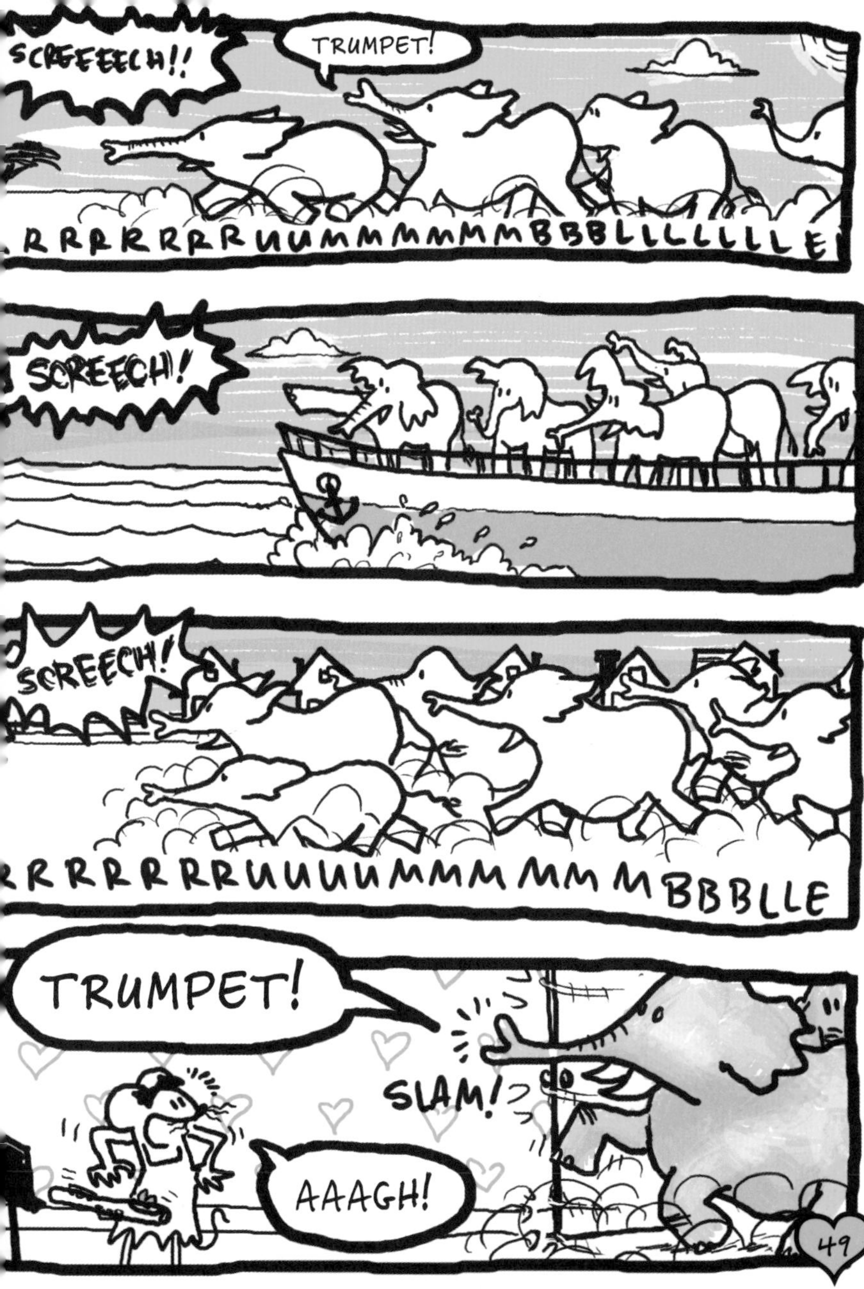
SCREEECH!!
TRUMPET!
RRRRRRRUUUMMMMMMBBBLLLLLLLE
SCREECH!
SCREECH!
RRRRRRRUUUUMMMMMMMBBBLLE
TRUMPET!
SLAM!
AAAGH!

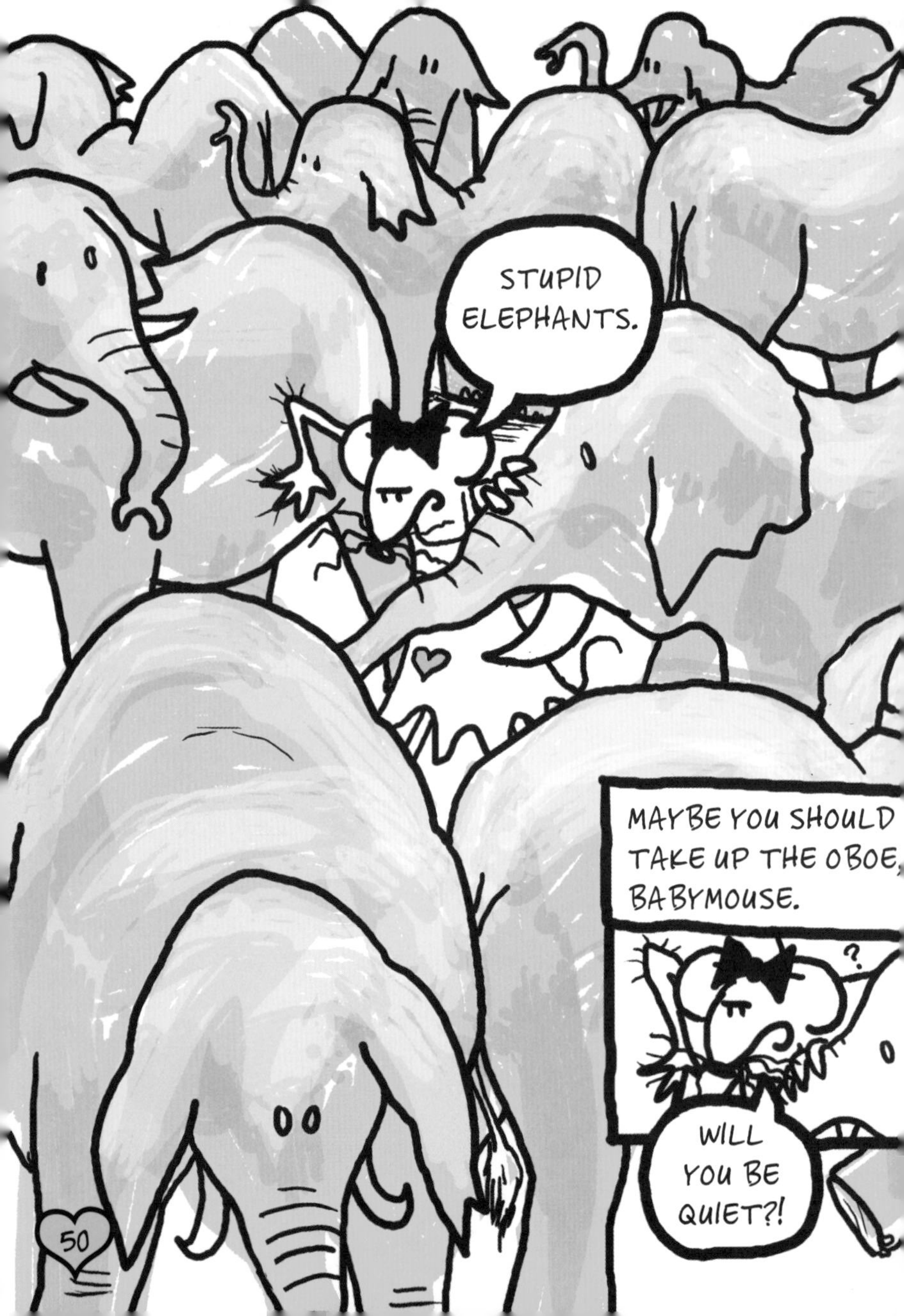
STUPID ELEPHANTS.
MAYBE YOU SHOULD TAKE UP THE OBOE, BABYMOUSE.
WILL YOU BE QUIET?!

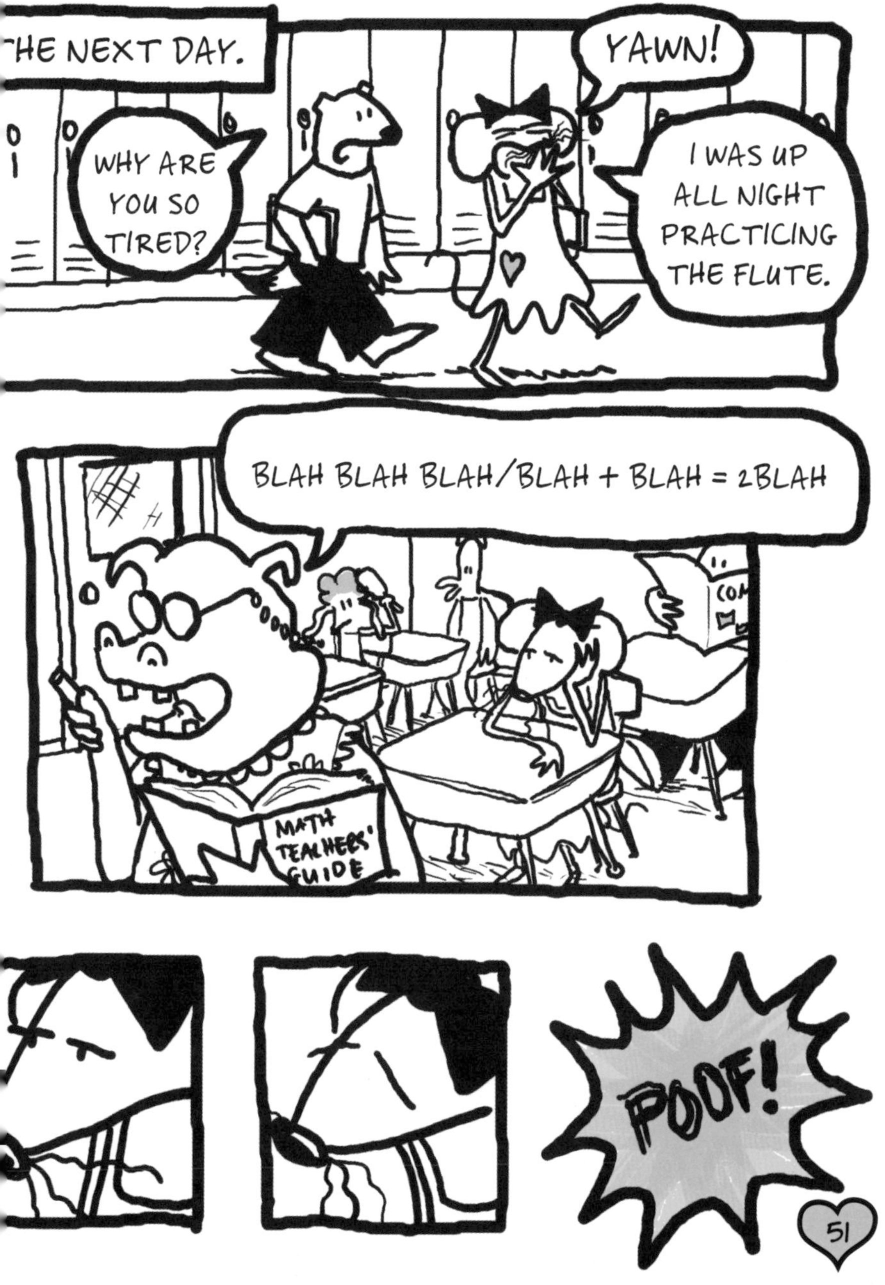
THE NEXT DAY.
WHY ARE YOU SO TIRED?
YAWN!
I WAS UP ALL NIGHT PRACTICING THE FLUTE.
BLAH BLAH BLAH/BLAH + BLAH = 2BLAH
MATH TEACHERS' GUIDE
POOF!

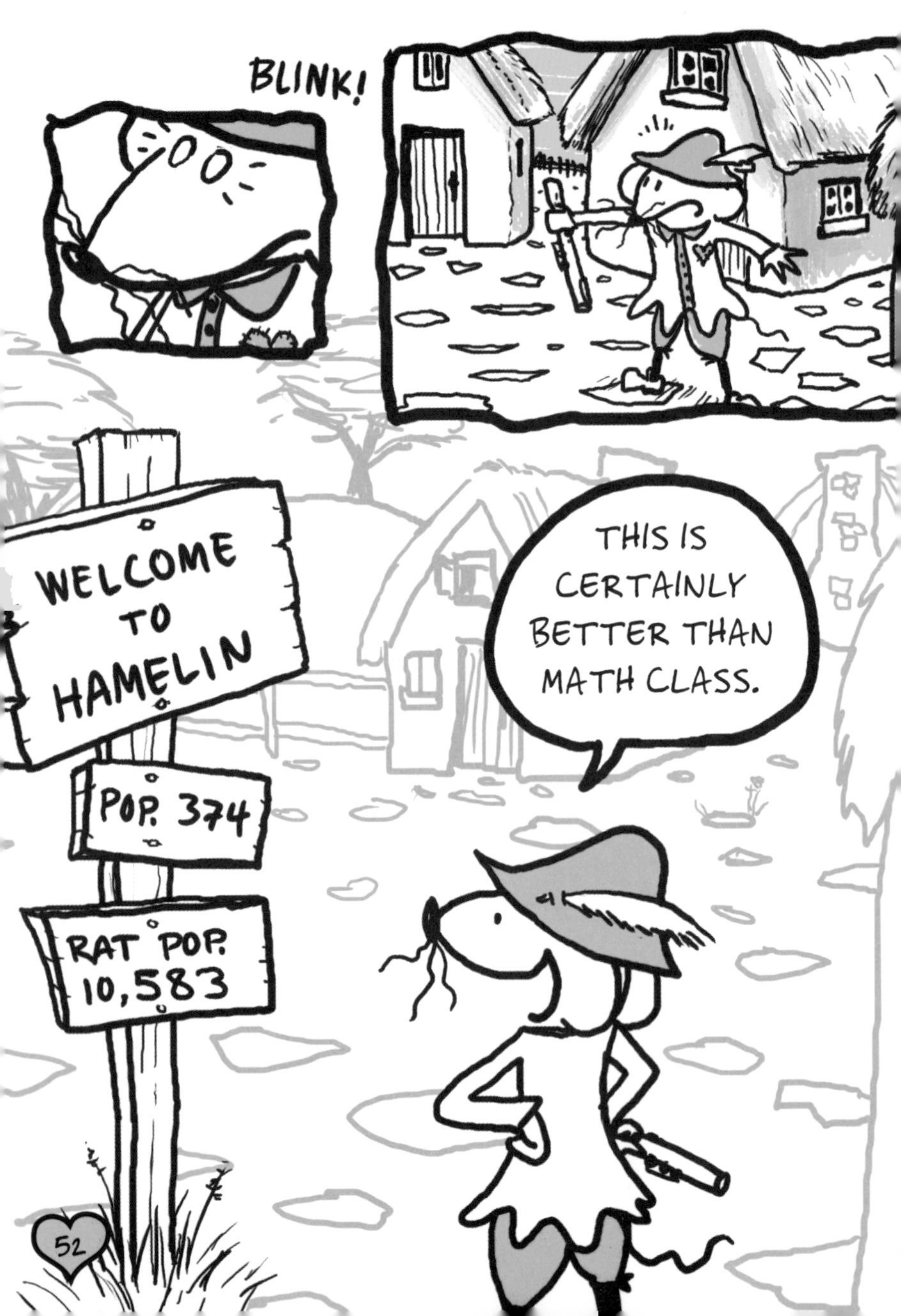
BLINK!
WELCOME TO HAMELIN
POP. 374
RAT POP. 10,583
THIS IS CERTAINLY BETTER THAN MATH CLASS.

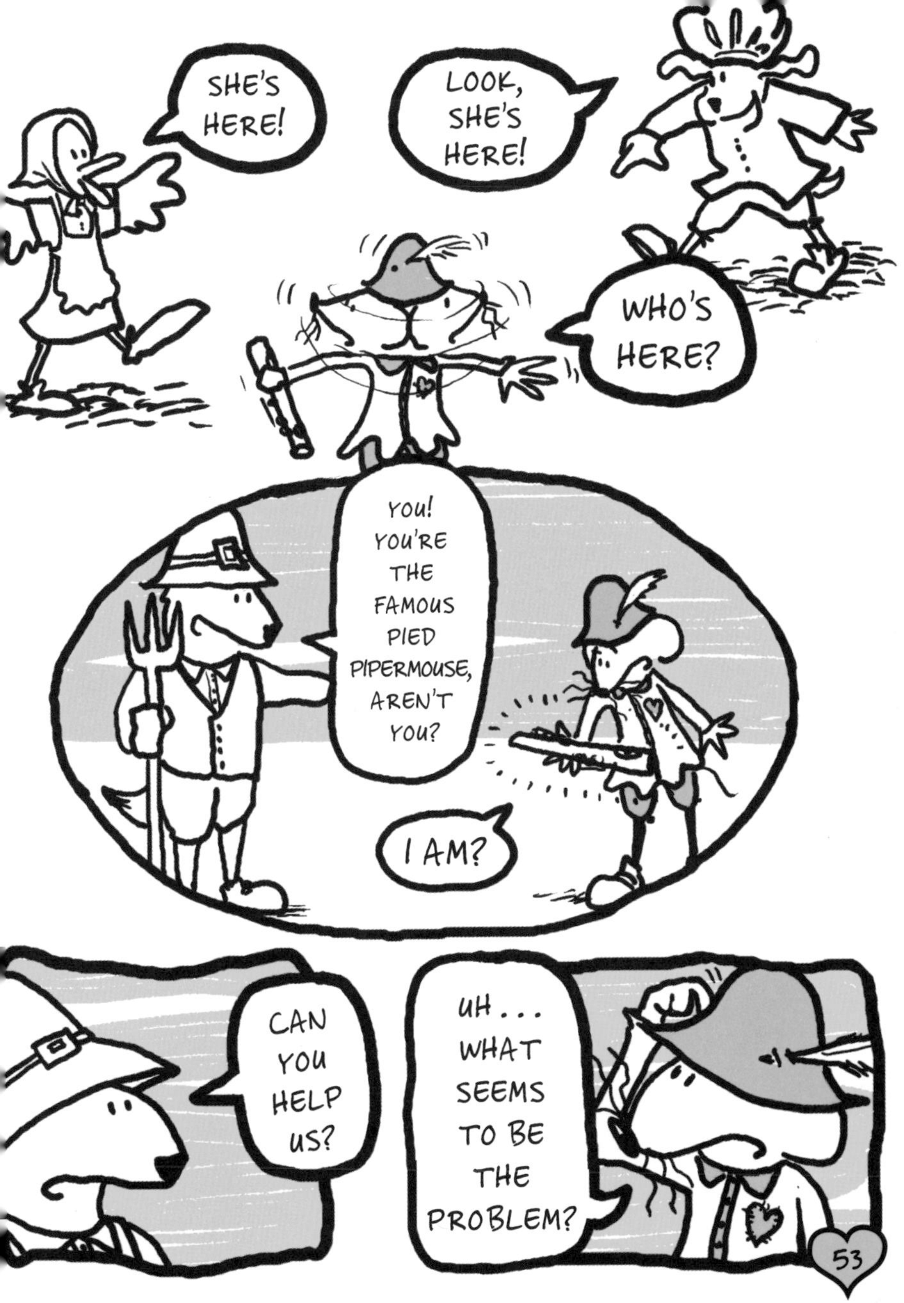
SHE'S HERE!
LOOK, SHE'S HERE!
WHO'S HERE?
YOU! YOU'RE THE FAMOUS PIED PIPERMOUSE, AREN'T YOU?
I AM?
CAN YOU HELP US?
UH . . . WHAT SEEMS TO BE THE PROBLEM?

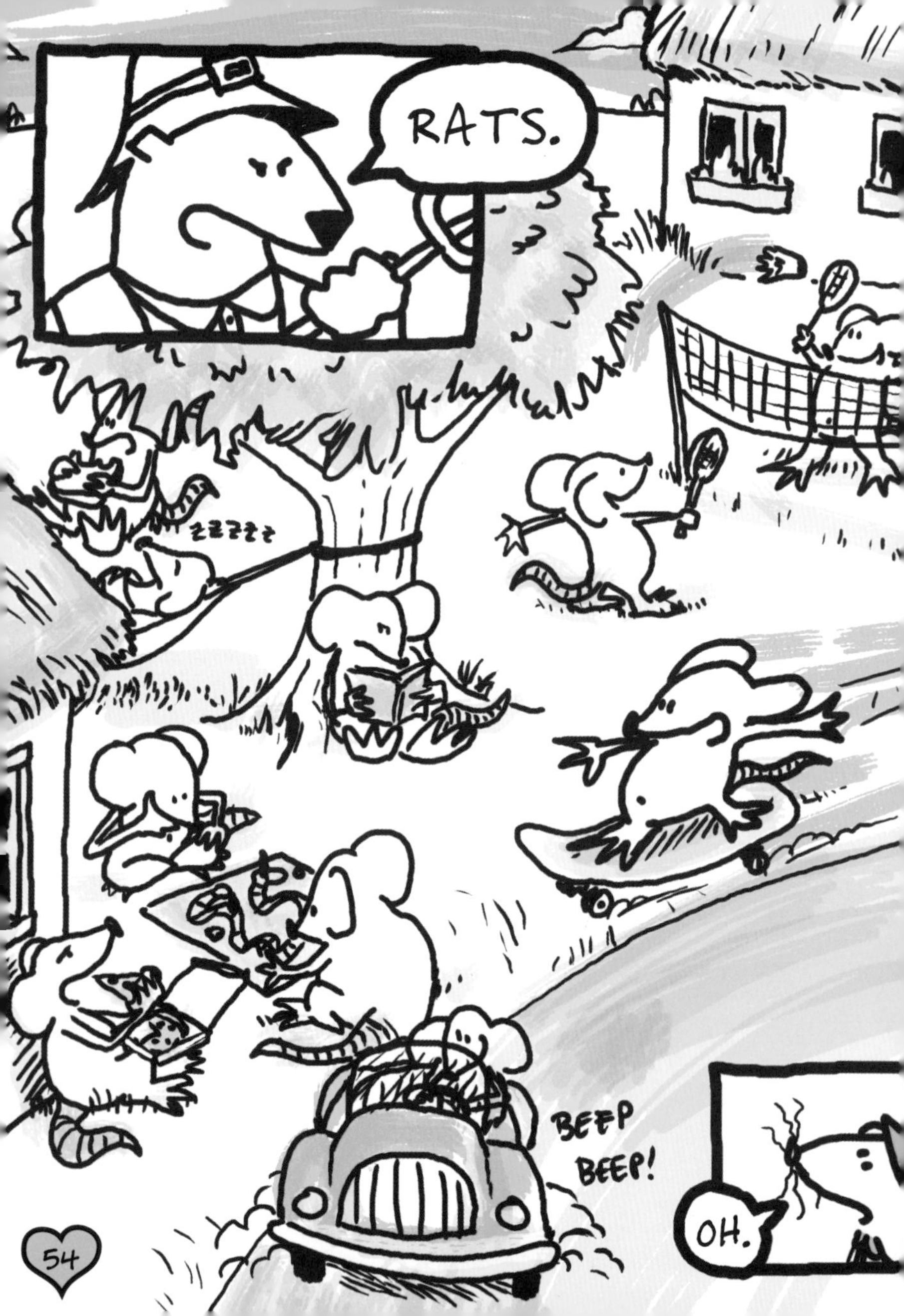
RATS.
ZZZZZZ
BEEP
BEEP!
OH.

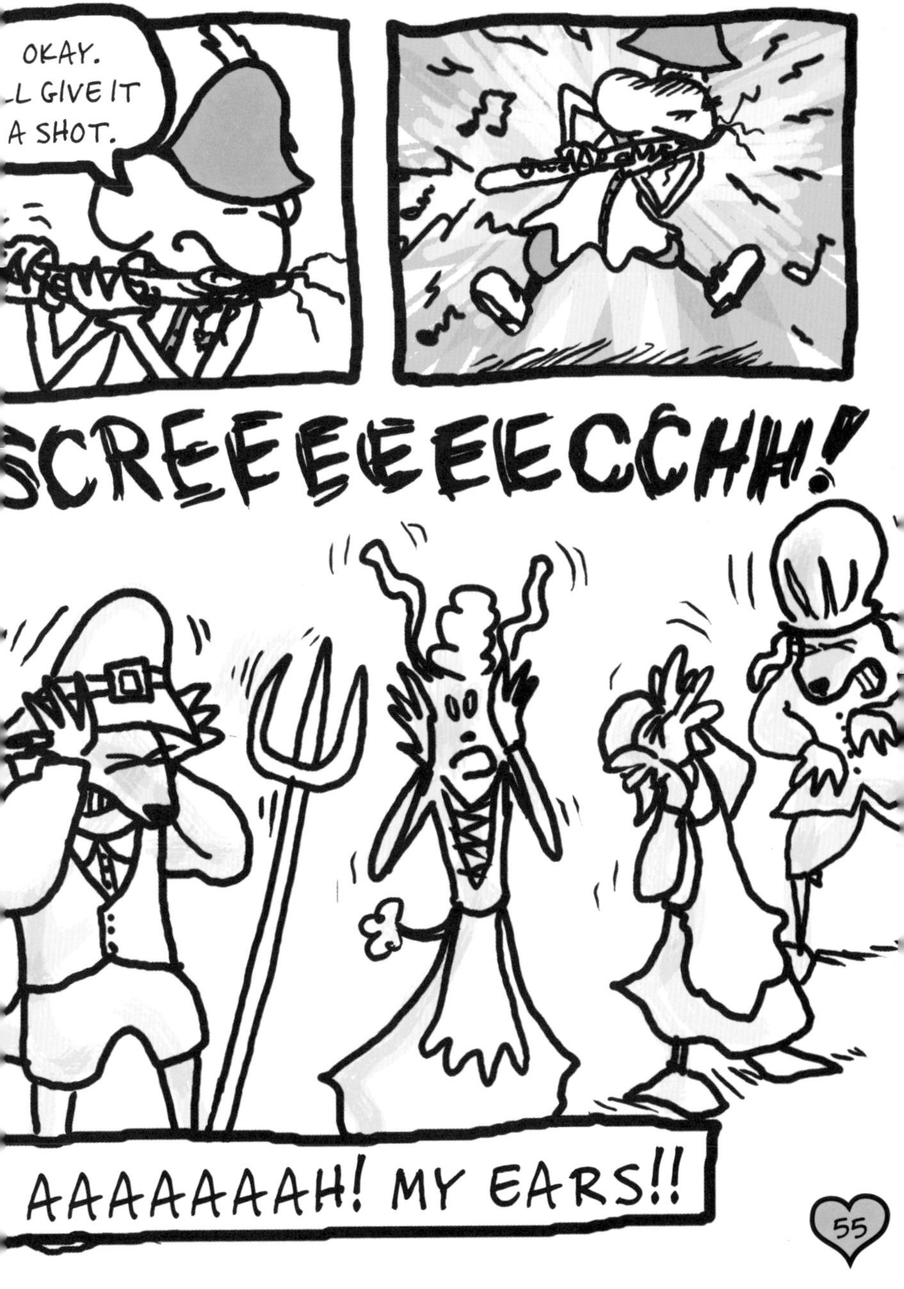
OKAY.
-LL GIVE IT
A SHOT.
SCREEEEEEEECCHH!
AAAAAAAH! MY EARS!!

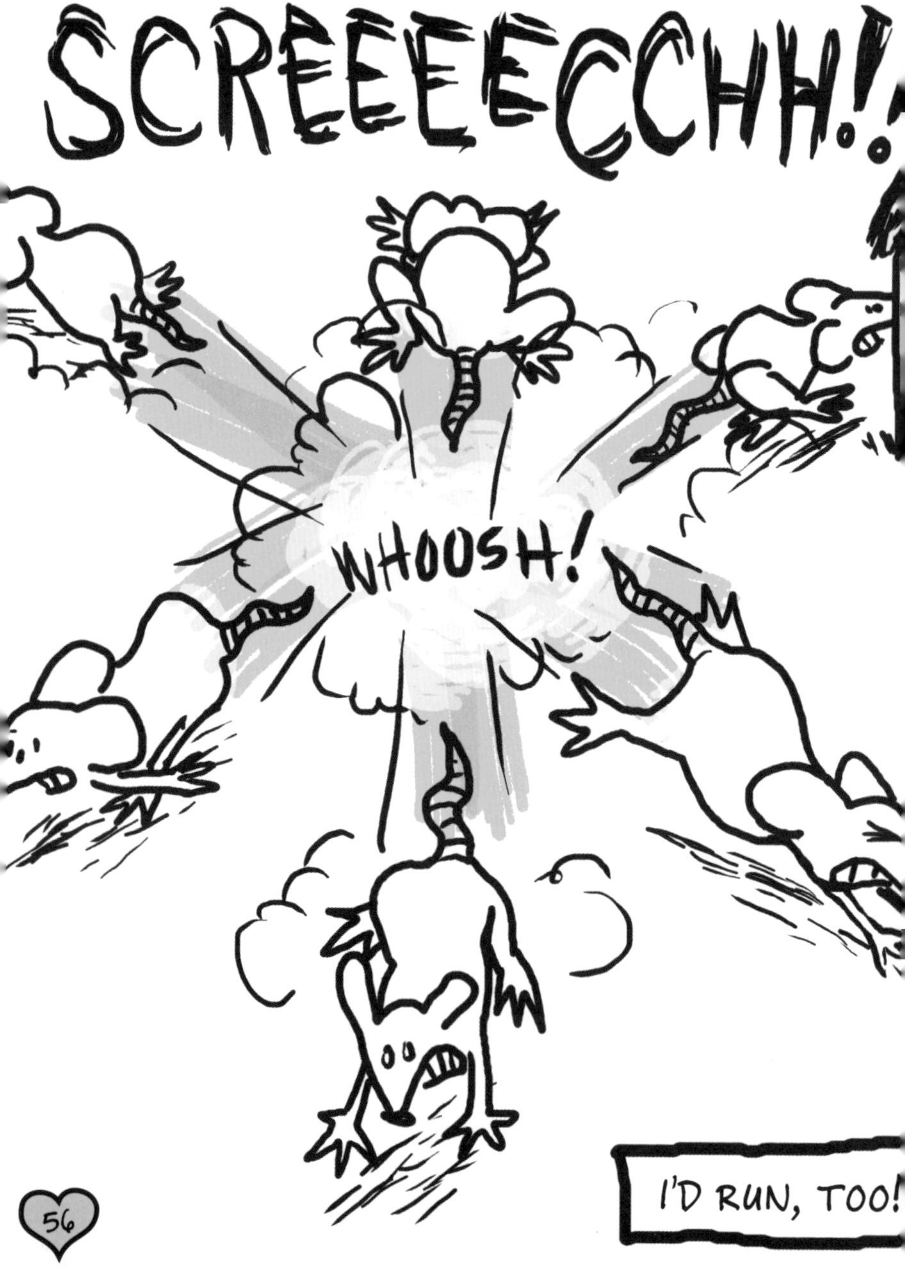
SCREEEECCHH!!
WHOOSH!
I'D RUN, TOO!

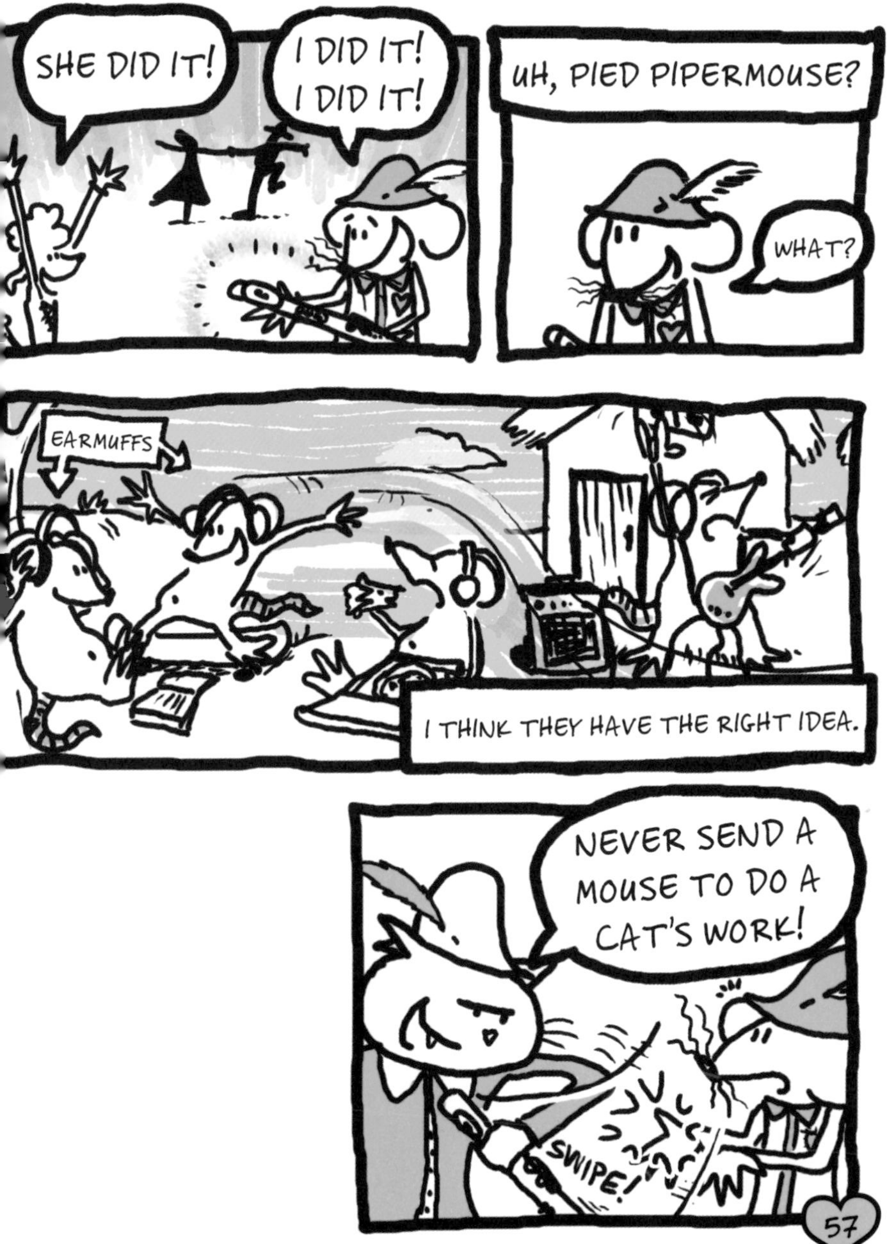

SHE DID IT!
I DID IT! I DID IT!
UH, PIED PIPERMOUSE?
WHAT?
EARMUFFS
I THINK THEY HAVE THE RIGHT IDEA.
NEVER SEND A MOUSE TO DO A CAT'S WORK!
SWIPE!

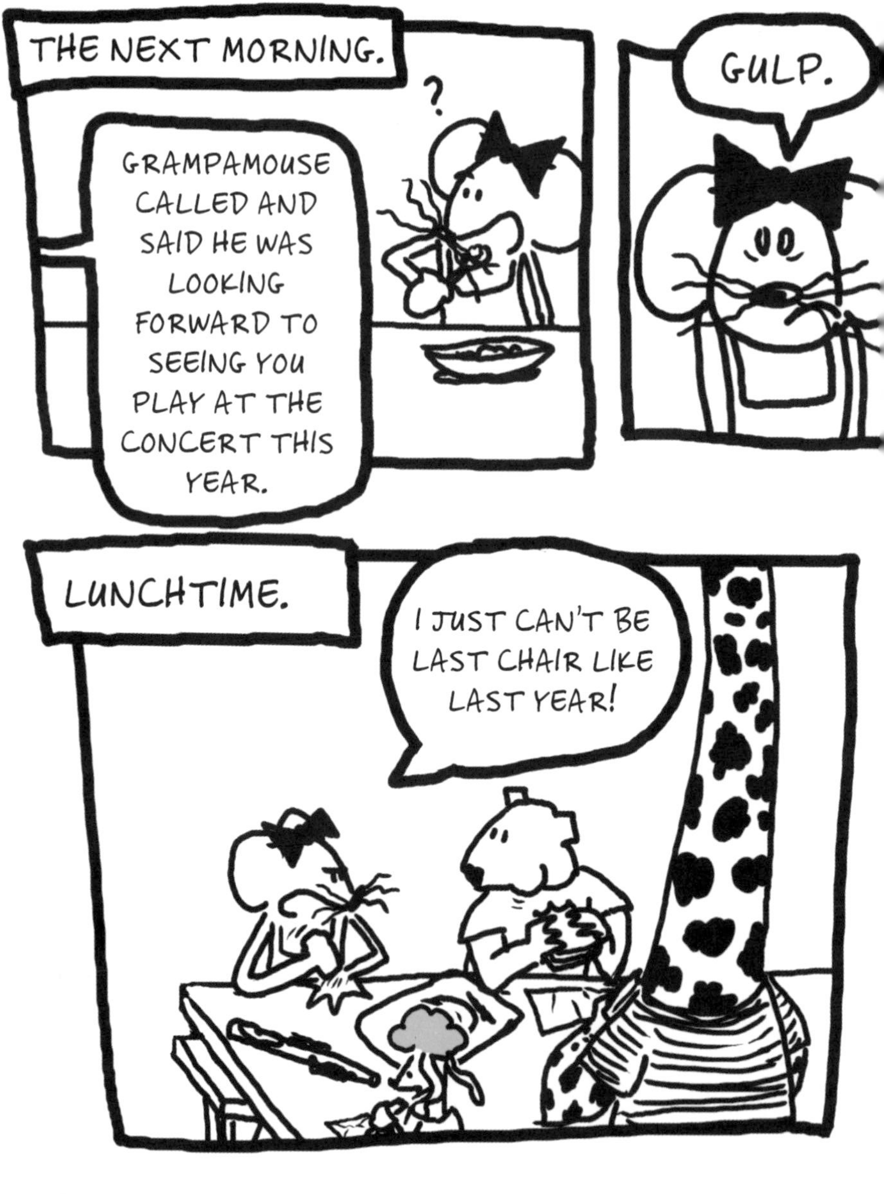
THE NEXT MORNING.
GRAMPAMOUSE CALLED AND SAID HE WAS LOOKING FORWARD TO SEEING YOU PLAY AT THE CONCERT THIS YEAR.
GULP.
LUNCHTIME.
I JUST CAN'T BE LAST CHAIR LIKE LAST YEAR!

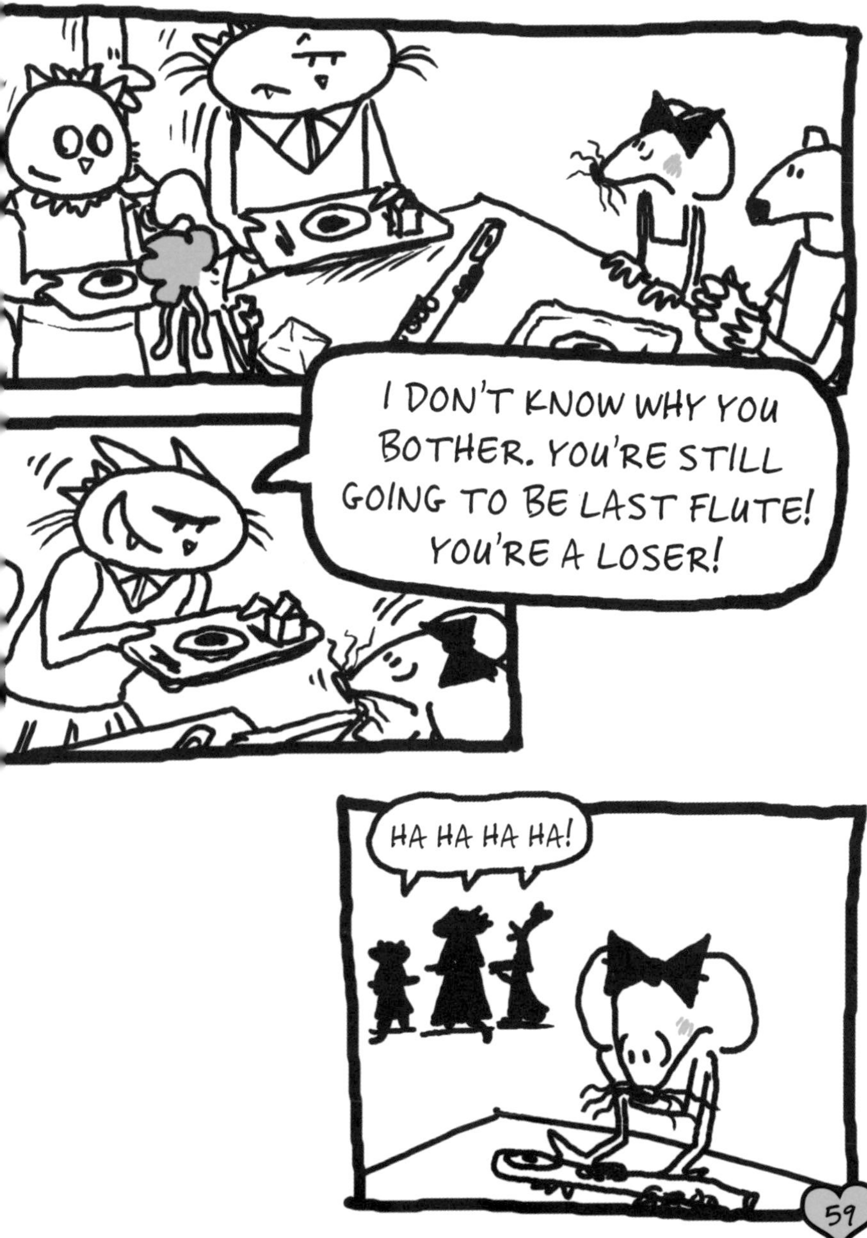
I DON'T KNOW WHY YOU BOTHER. YOU'RE STILL GOING TO BE LAST FLUTE! YOU'RE A LOSER!
HA HA HA HA!

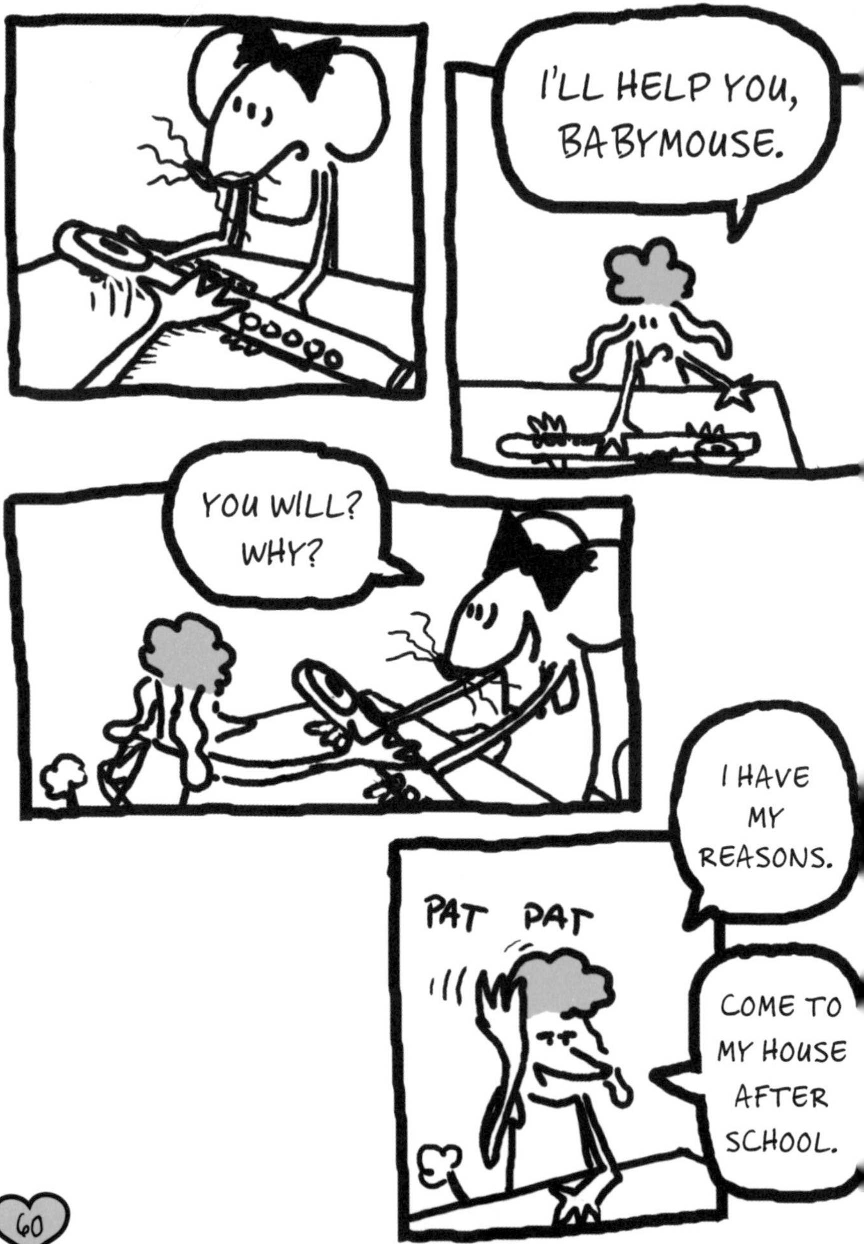
I'LL HELP YOU, BABYMOUSE.
YOU WILL? WHY?
I HAVE MY REASONS.
PAT PAT
COME TO MY HOUSE AFTER SCHOOL.

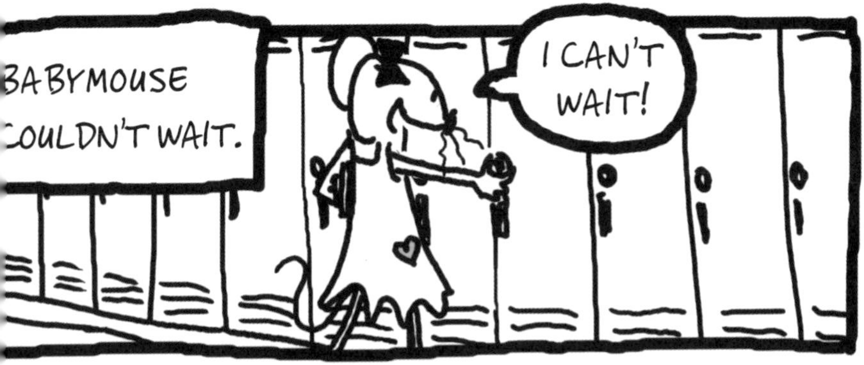
BABYMOUSE COULDN'T WAIT.
I CAN'T WAIT!

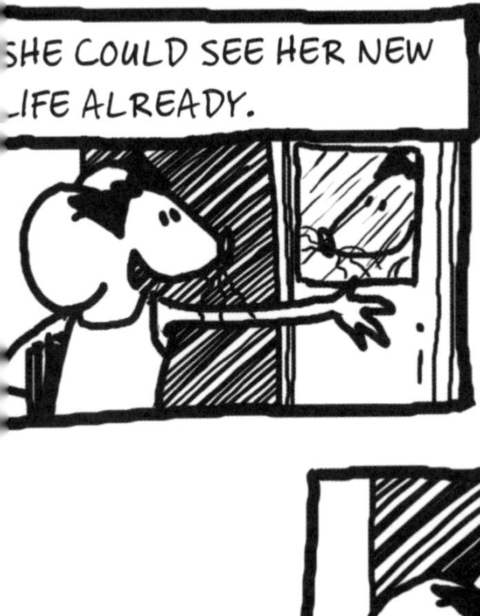
SHE COULD SEE HER NEW LIFE ALREADY.

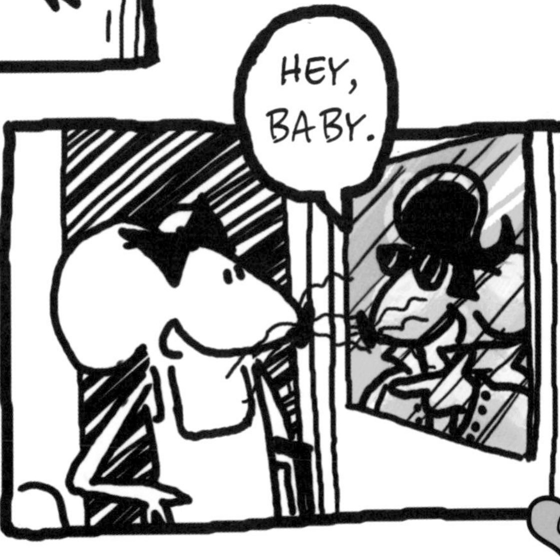
HEY, BABY.

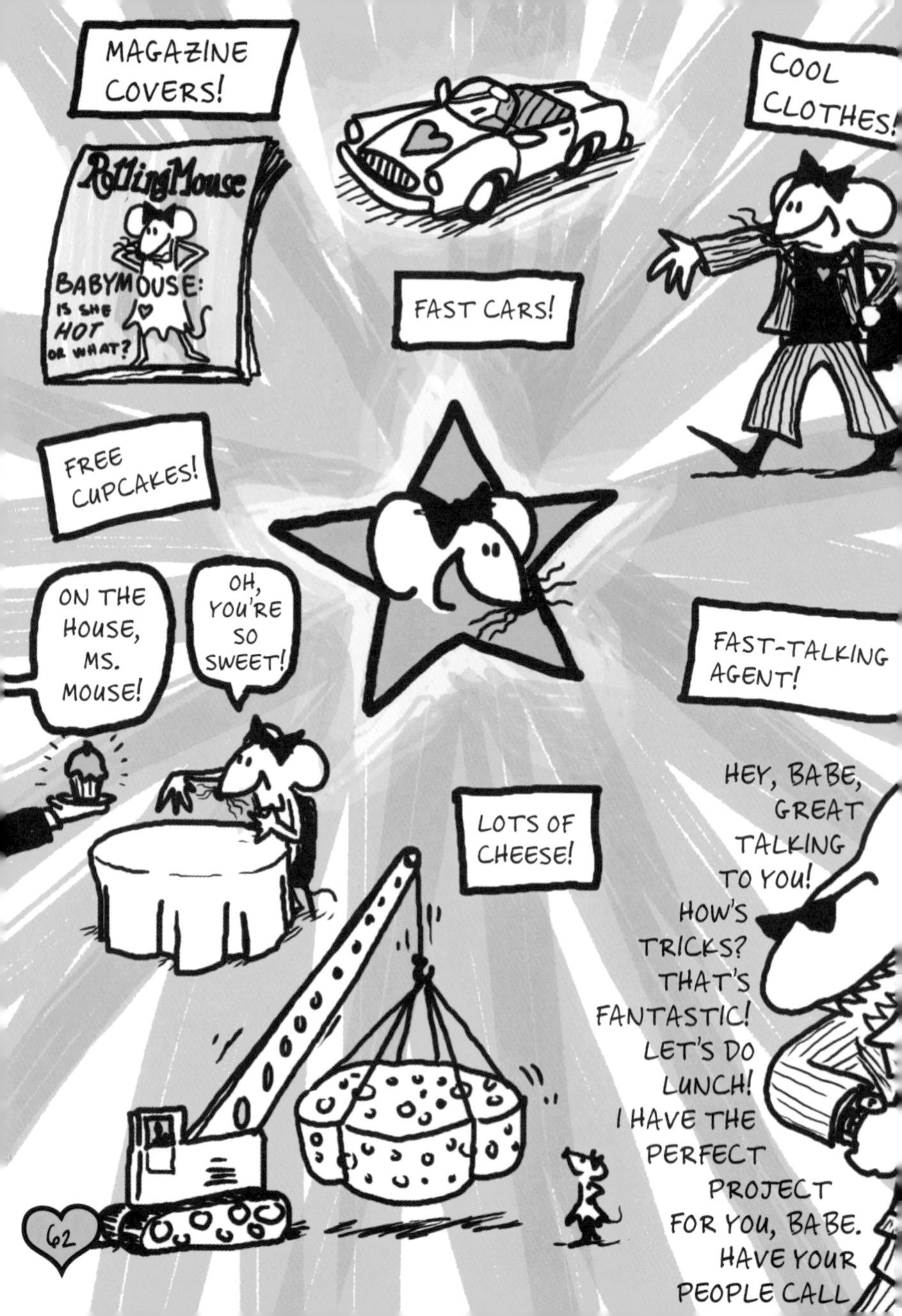
MAGAZINE COVERS!
RollingMouse
BABYMOUSE: IS SHE HOT OR WHAT?
FAST CARS!
COOL CLOTHES!
FREE CUPCAKES!
ON THE HOUSE, MS. MOUSE!
OH, YOU'RE SO SWEET!
FAST-TALKING AGENT!
LOTS OF CHEESE!
HEY, BABE, GREAT TALKING TO YOU! HOW'S TRICKS? THAT'S FANTASTIC! LET'S DO LUNCH! I HAVE THE PERFECT PROJECT FOR YOU, BABE. HAVE YOUR PEOPLE CALL

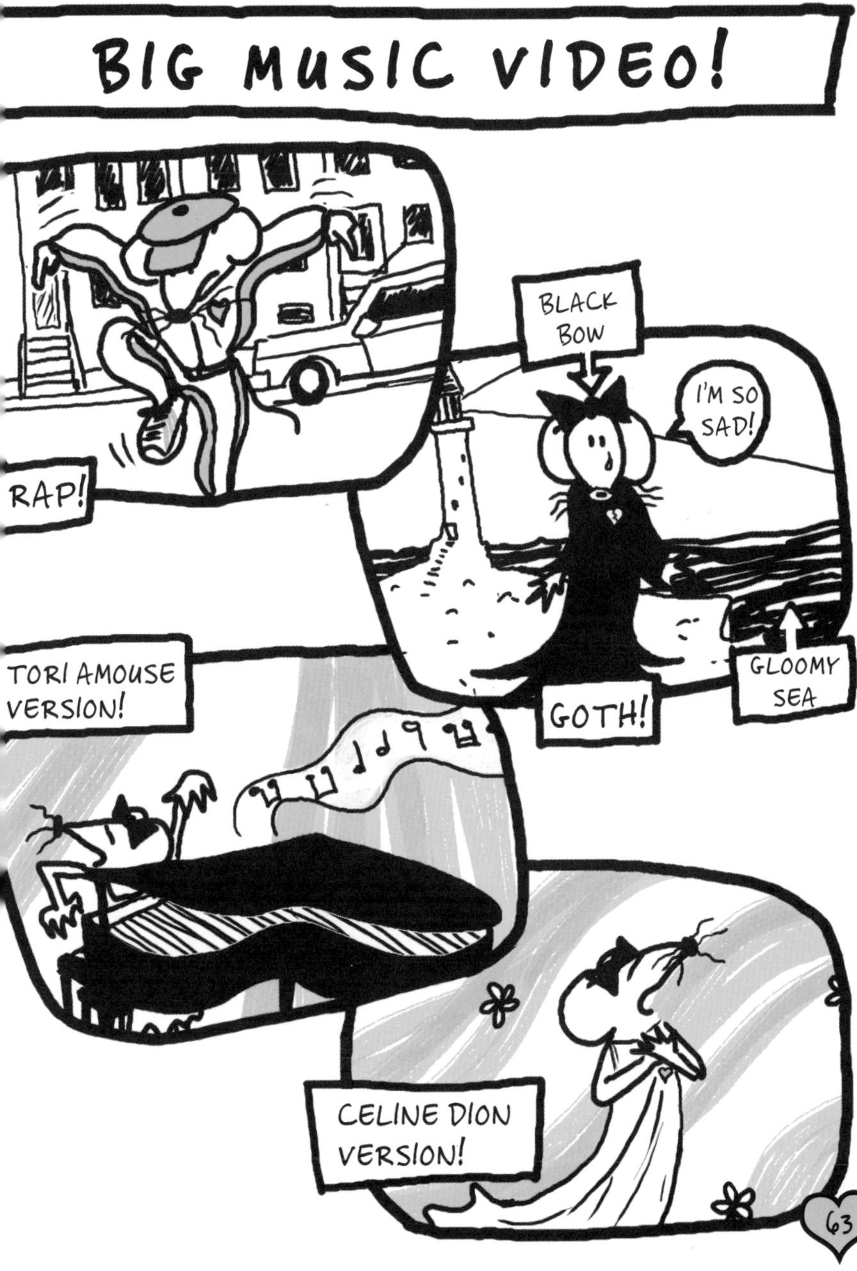
BIG MUSIC VIDEO!
RAP!
BLACK BOW
I'M SO SAD!
GOTH!
GLOOMY SEA
TORI AMOUSE VERSION!
CELINE DION VERSION!

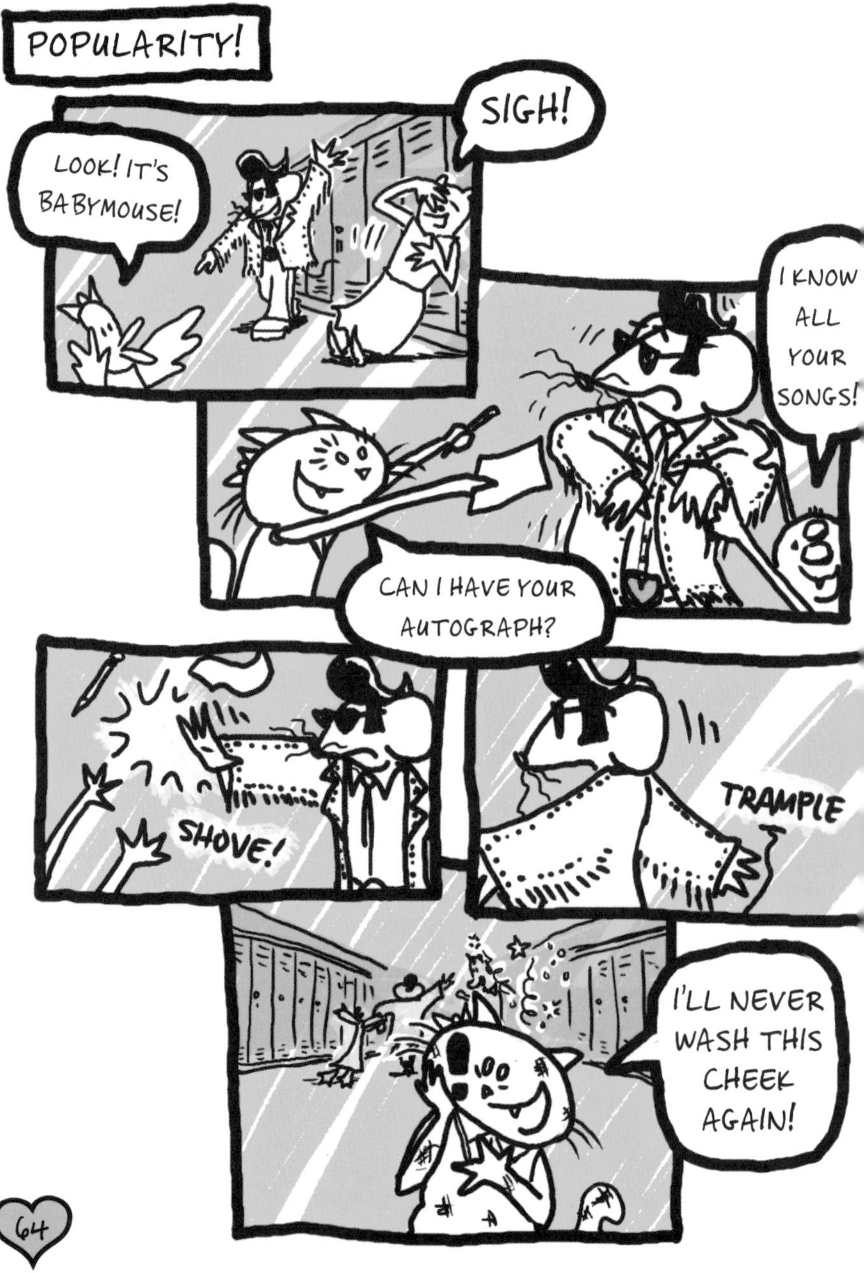
POPULARITY!
LOOK! IT'S BABYMOUSE!
SIGH!
I KNOW ALL YOUR SONGS!
CAN I HAVE YOUR AUTOGRAPH?
SHOVE!
TRAMPLE
I'LL NEVER WASH THIS CHEEK AGAIN!

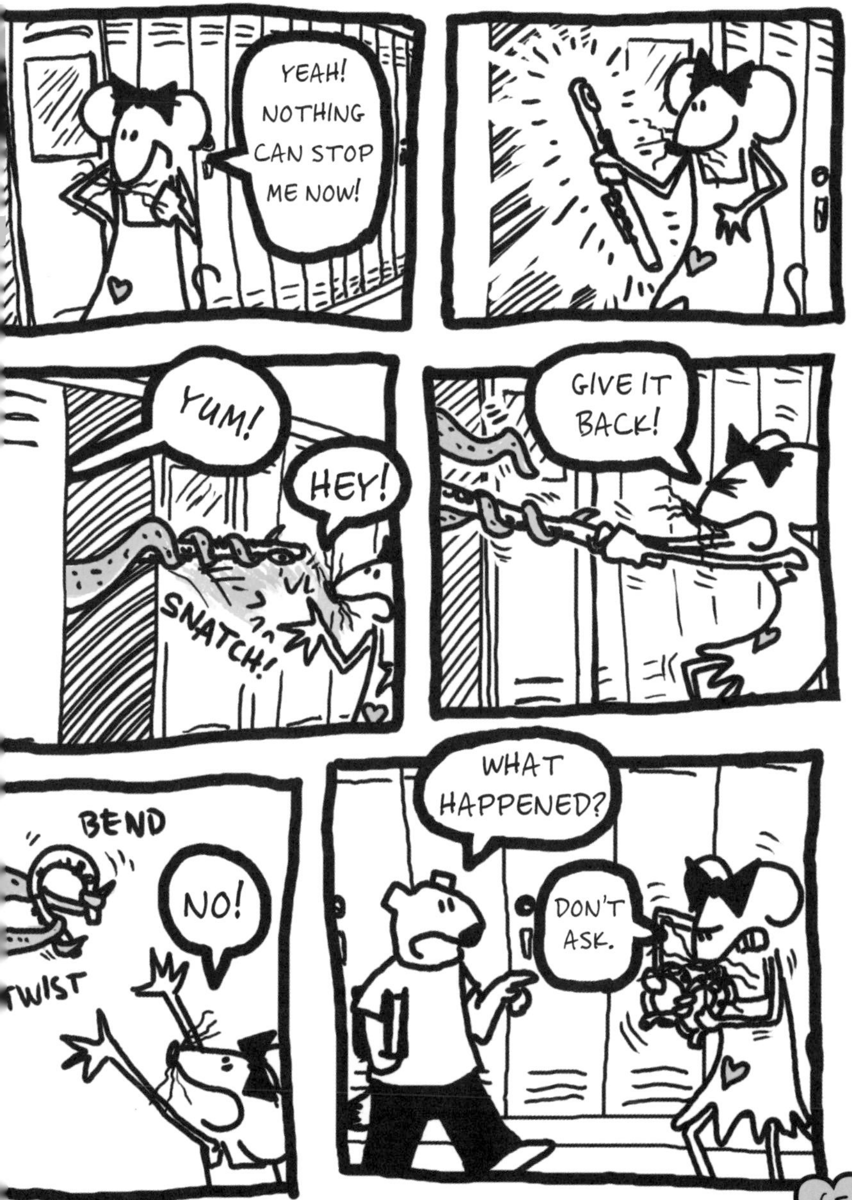
YEAH! NOTHING CAN STOP ME NOW!
YUM!
HEY!
SNATCH!
GIVE IT BACK!
BEND
TWIST
NO!
WHAT HAPPENED?
DON'T ASK.

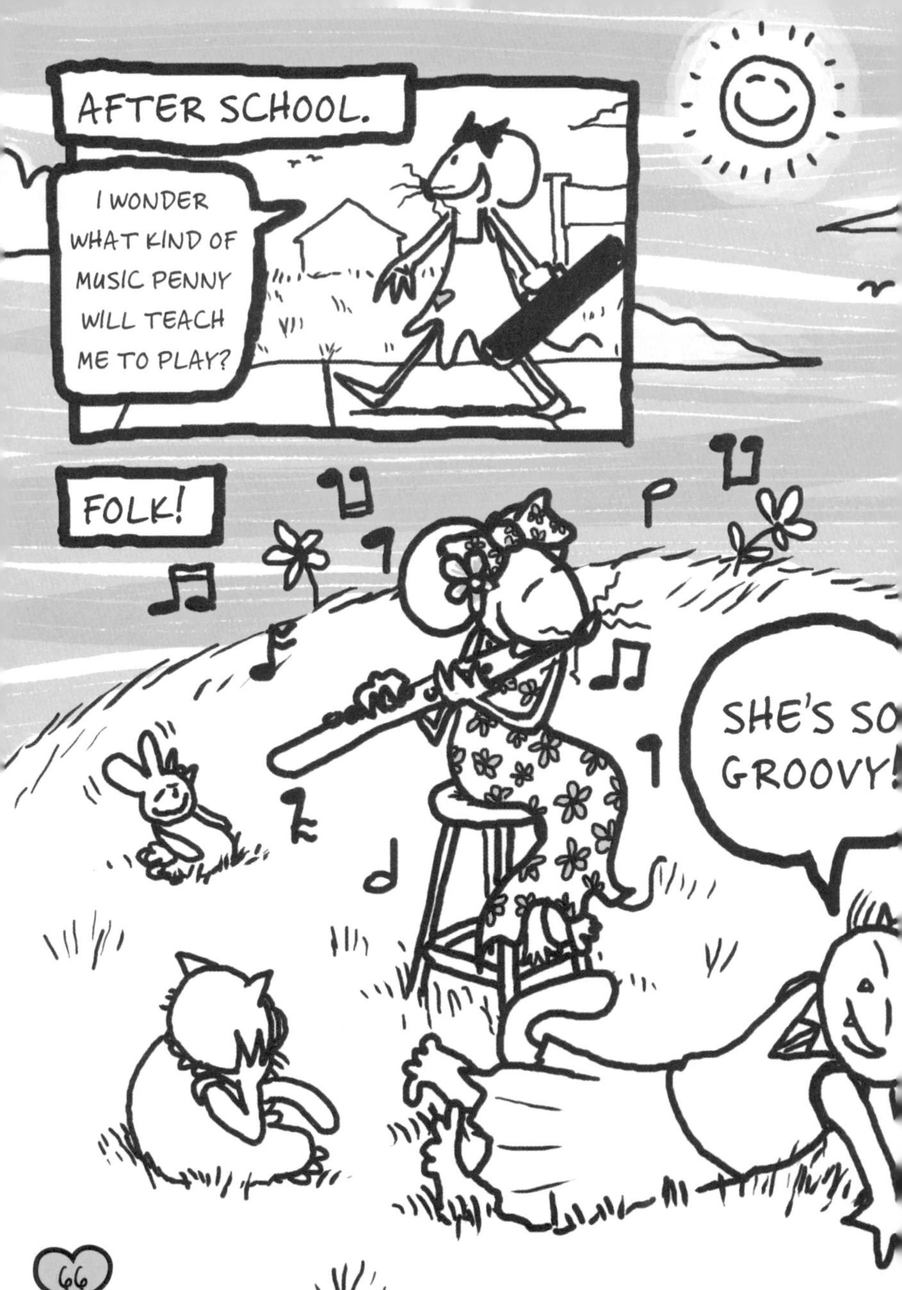
AFTER SCHOOL.
I WONDER WHAT KIND OF MUSIC PENNY WILL TEACH ME TO PLAY?
FOLK!
SHE'S SO GROOVY!

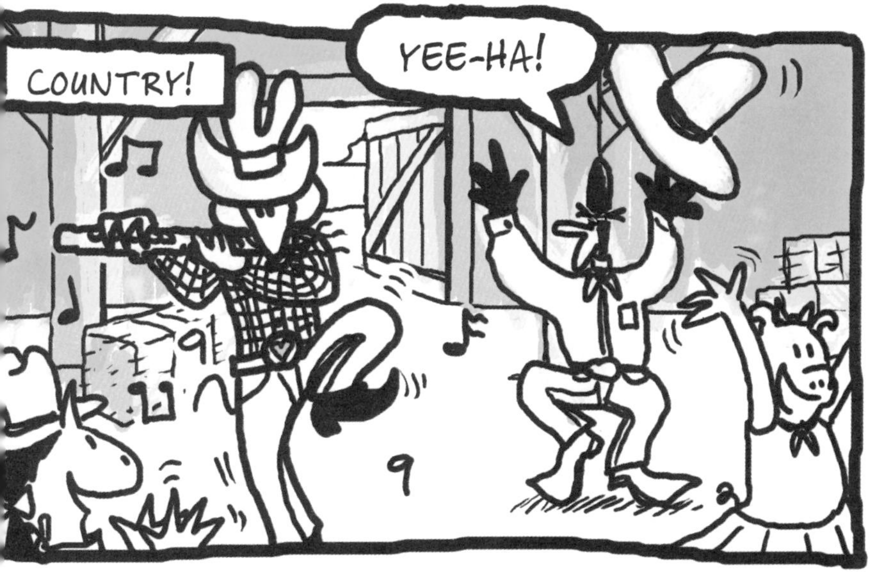
COUNTRY!
YEE-HA!

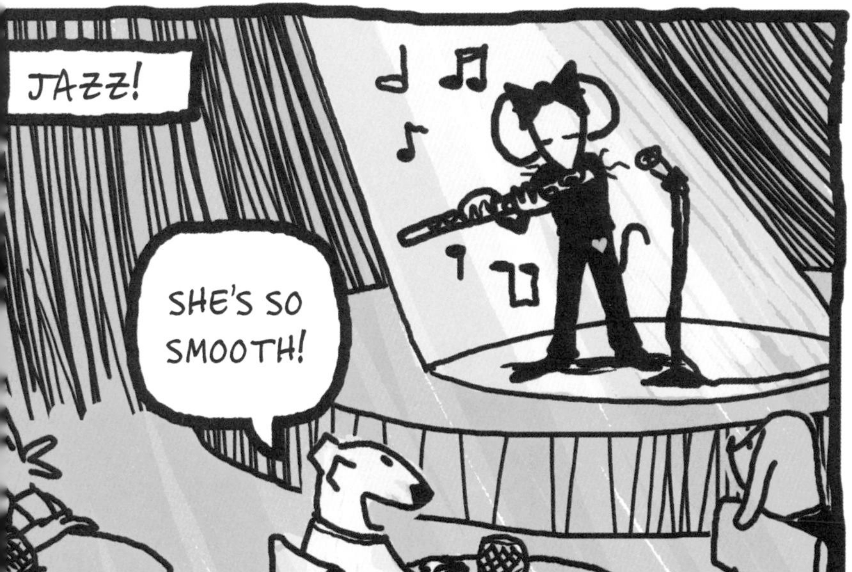
JAZZ!
SHE'S SO SMOOTH!

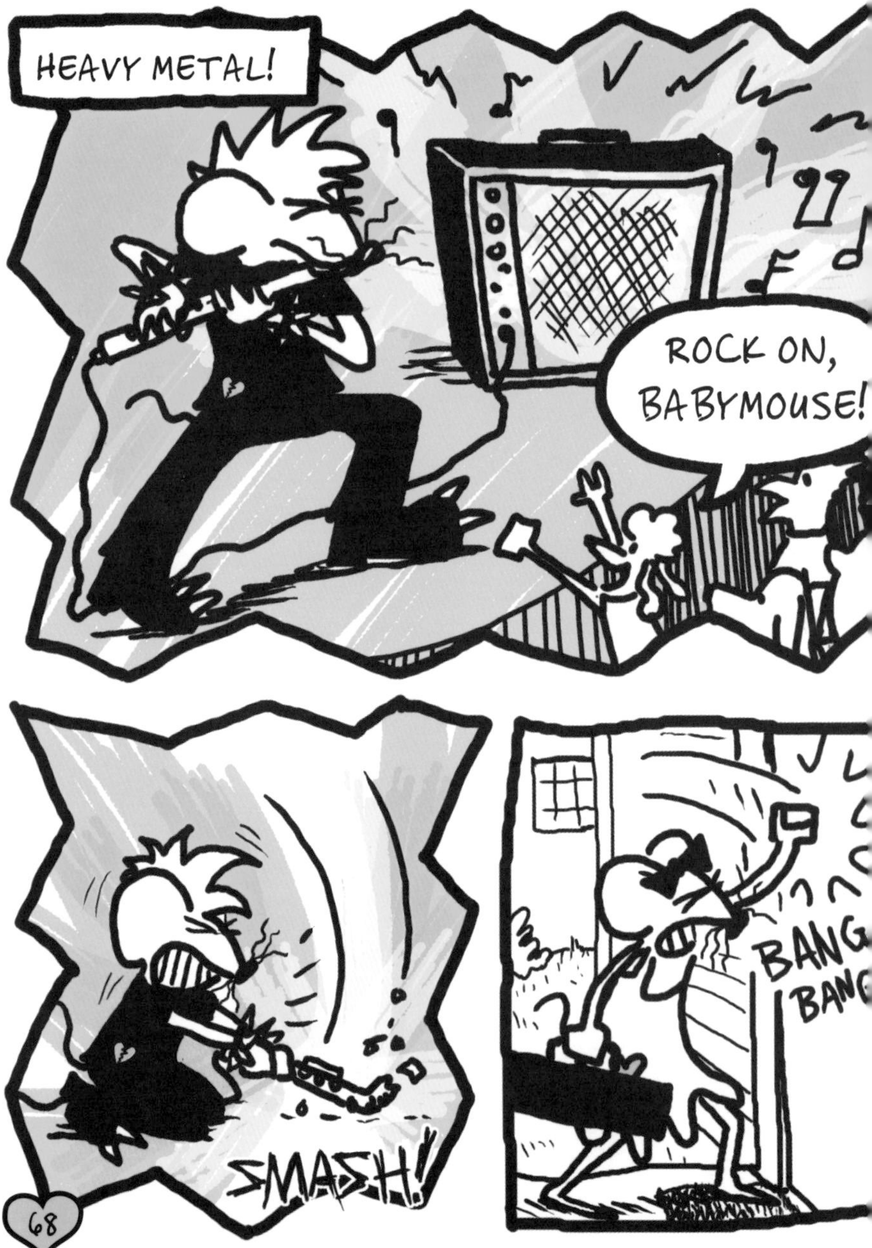
HEAVY METAL!
ROCK ON, BABYMOUSE!
SMASH!
BANG
BANG

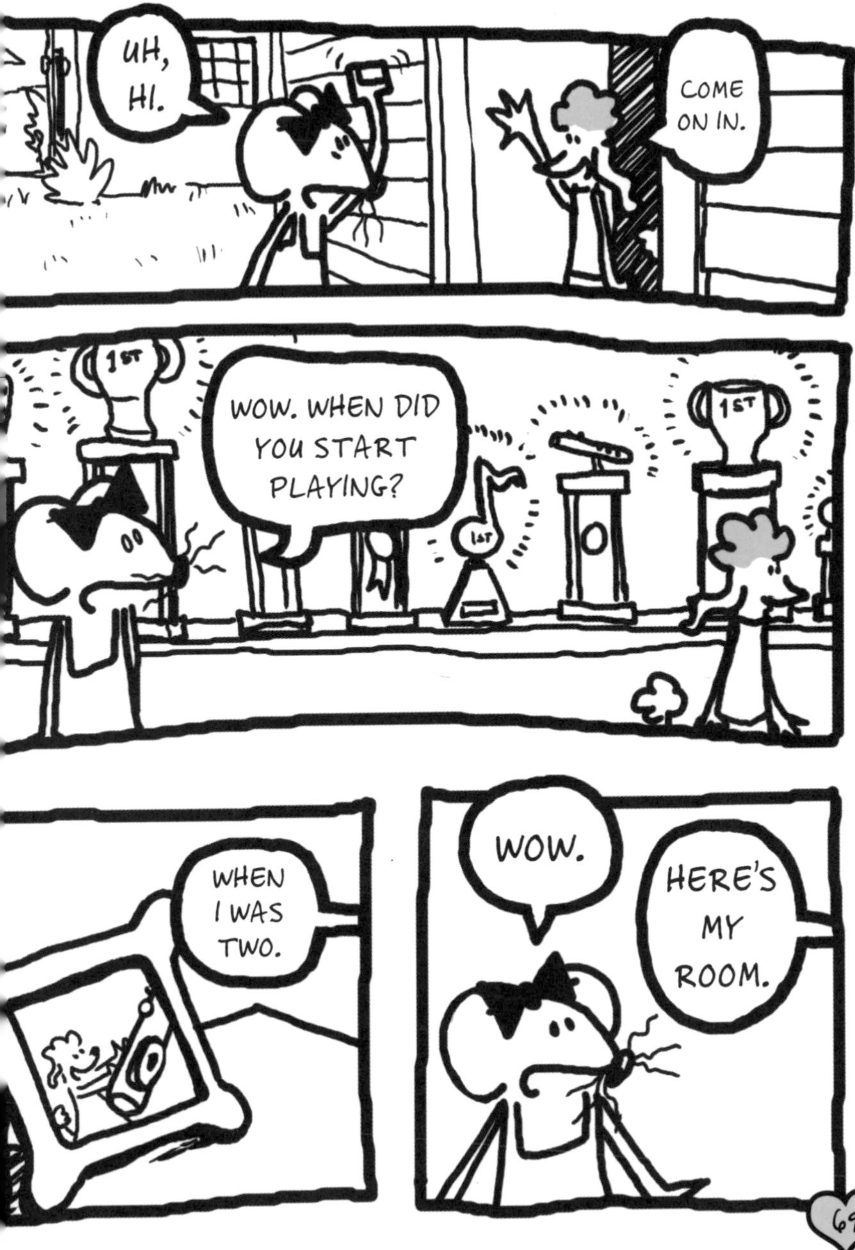
UH, HI.
COME ON IN.
1ST
WOW. WHEN DID YOU START PLAYING?
1ST
1ST
WHEN I WAS TWO.
WOW.
HERE'S MY ROOM.

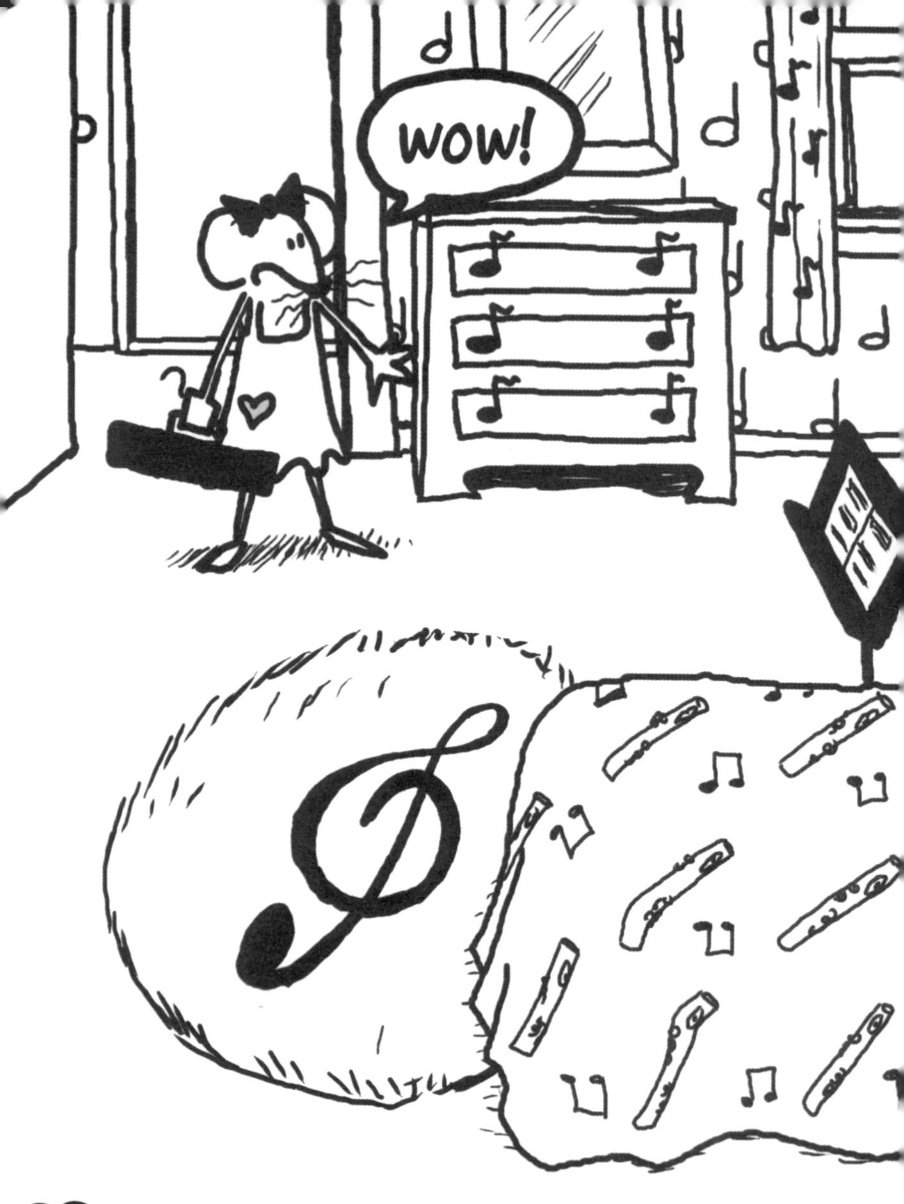
WOW!

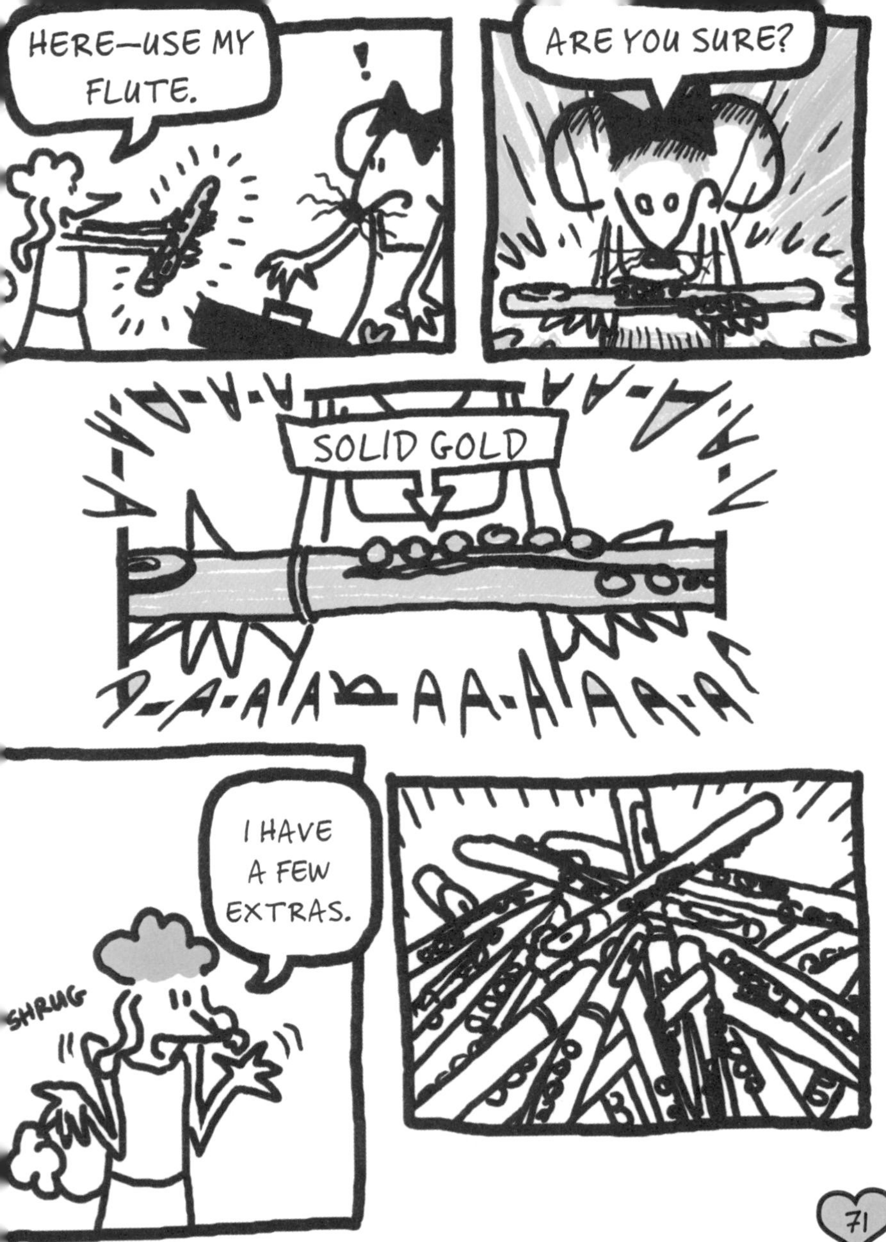
HERE—USE MY FLUTE.
!
ARE YOU SURE?
SOLID GOLD
I HAVE A FEW EXTRAS.
SHRUG

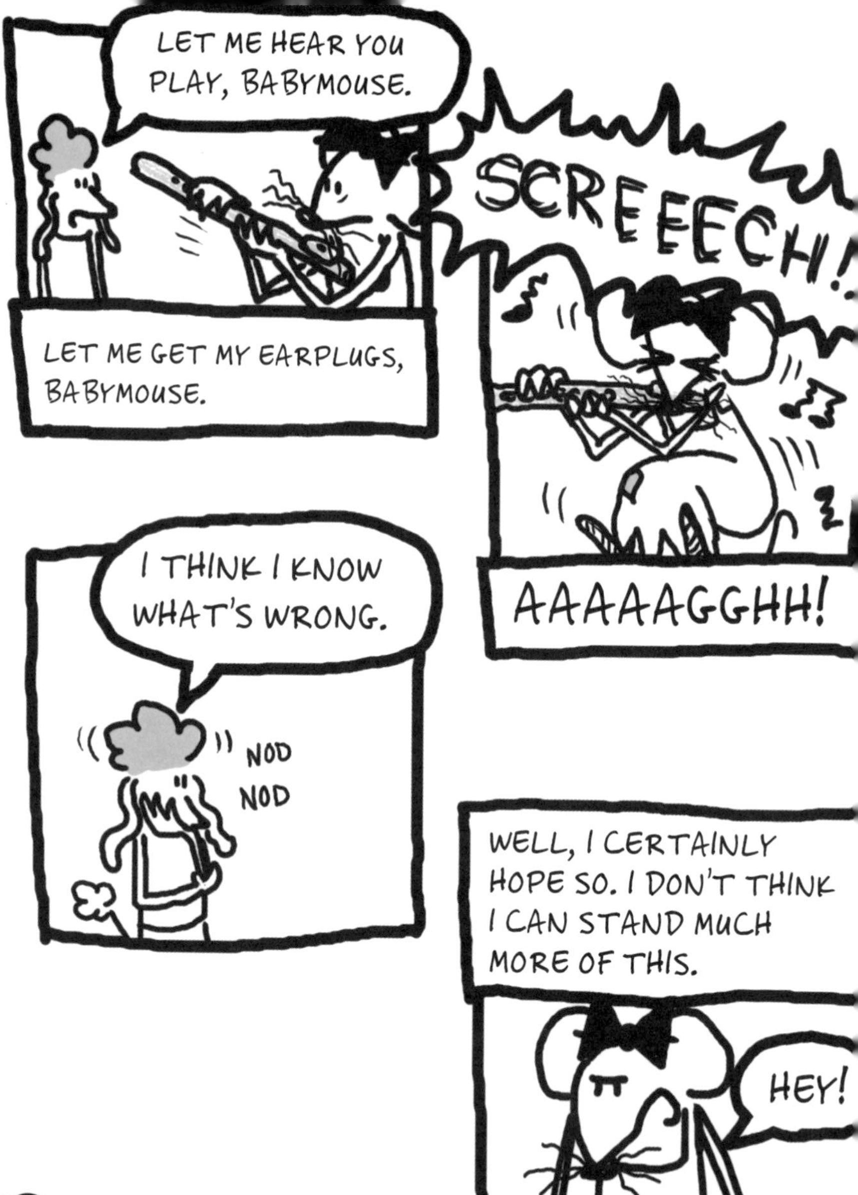
LET ME HEAR YOU PLAY, BABYMOUSE.
LET ME GET MY EARPLUGS, BABYMOUSE.
SCREEEECH!!
AAAAAGGHH!
I THINK I KNOW WHAT'S WRONG.
NOD
NOD
WELL, I CERTAINLY HOPE SO. I DON'T THINK I CAN STAND MUCH MORE OF THIS.
HEY!

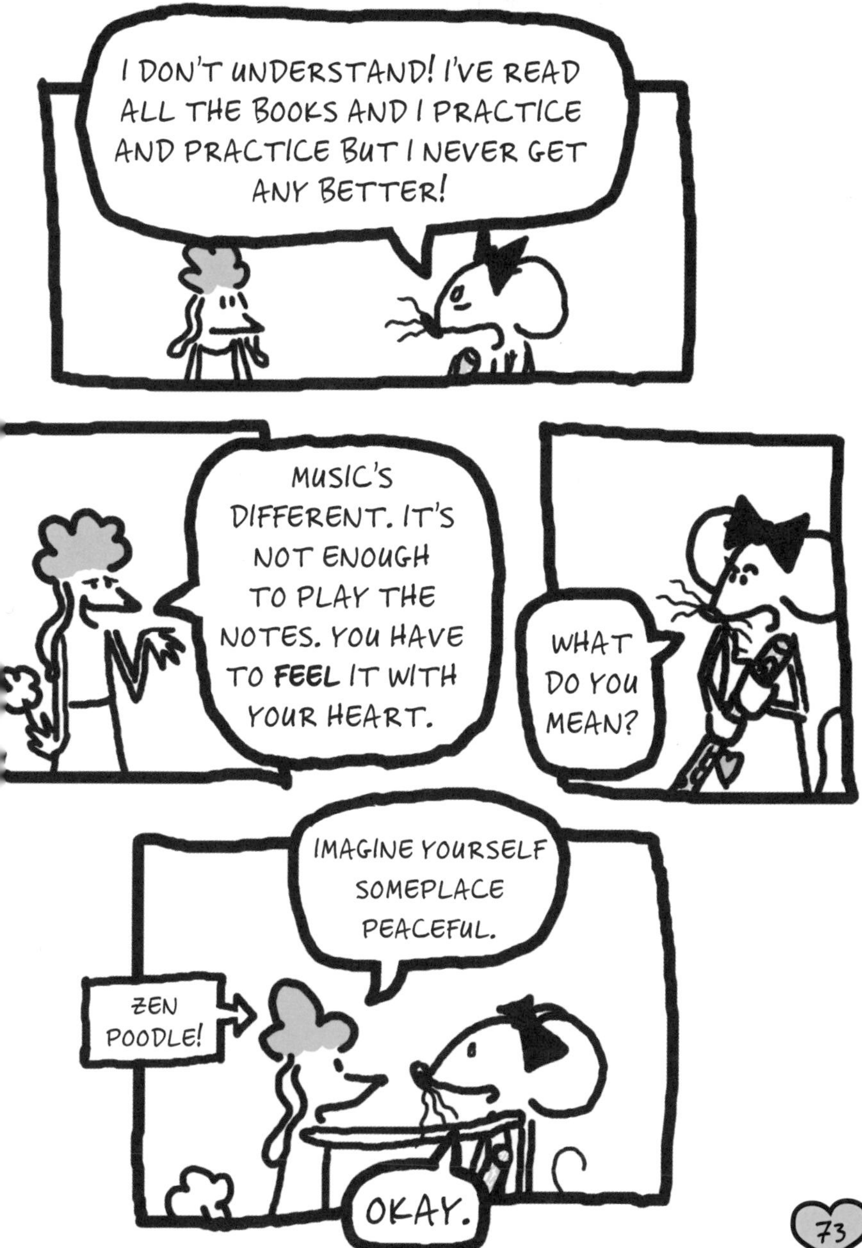

I DON'T UNDERSTAND! I'VE READ ALL THE BOOKS AND I PRACTICE AND PRACTICE BUT I NEVER GET ANY BETTER!
MUSIC'S DIFFERENT. IT'S NOT ENOUGH TO PLAY THE NOTES. YOU HAVE TO **FEEL** IT WITH YOUR HEART.
WHAT DO YOU MEAN?
IMAGINE YOURSELF SOMEPLACE PEACEFUL.
ZEN POODLE!
OKAY.

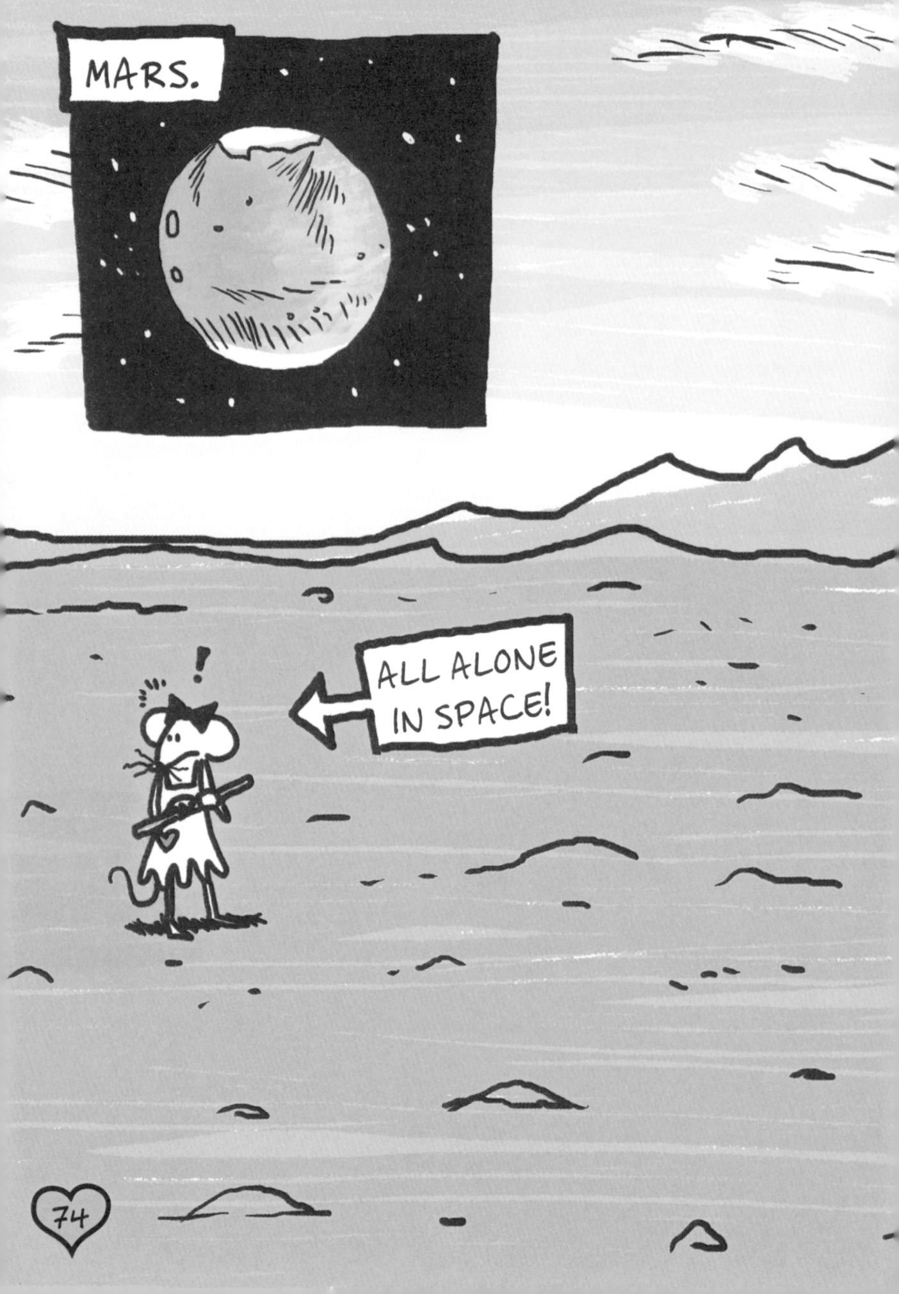
MARS.
ALL ALONE IN SPACE!
!

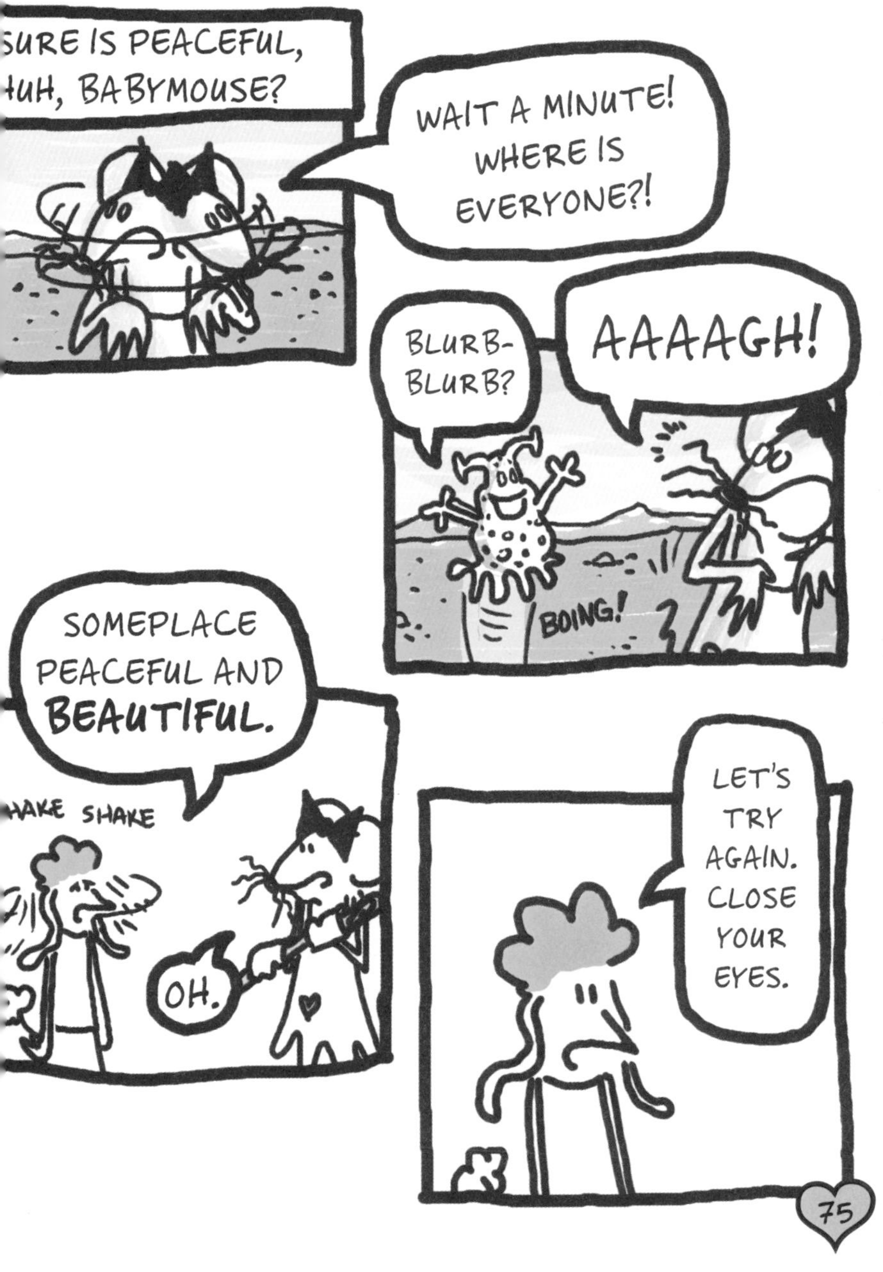
SURE IS PEACEFUL, HUH, BABYMOUSE?
WAIT A MINUTE! WHERE IS EVERYONE?!
BLURB-BLURB?
AAAAGH!
BOING!
SOMEPLACE PEACEFUL AND **BEAUTIFUL.**
SHAKE SHAKE
OH.
LET'S TRY AGAIN. CLOSE YOUR EYES.

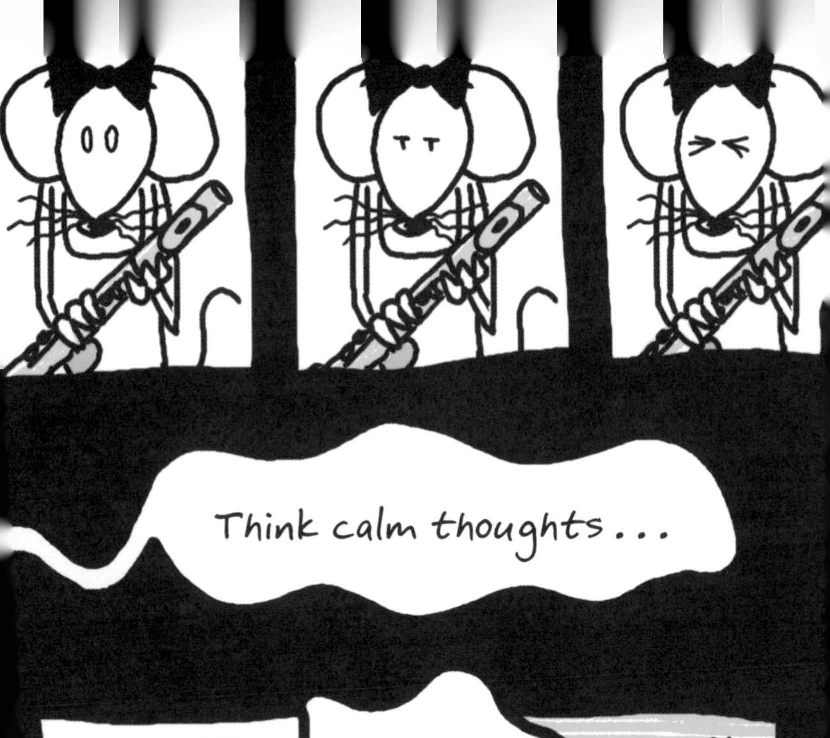
Think calm thoughts . . .
Where are you?
BLINK!

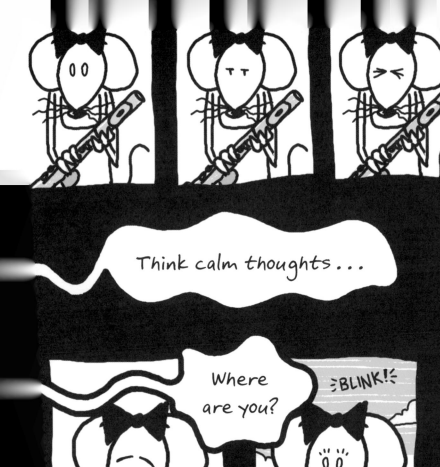

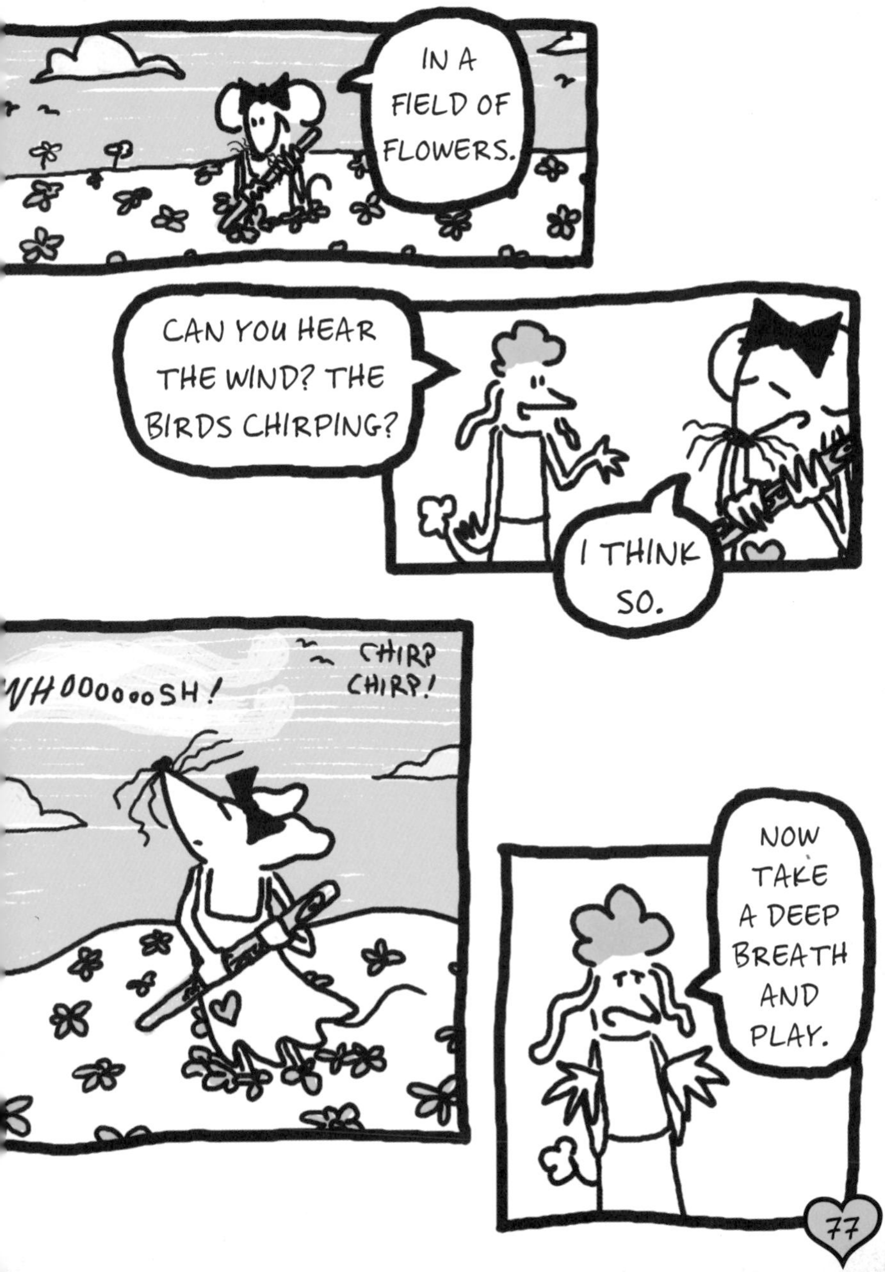
IN A FIELD OF FLOWERS.
CAN YOU HEAR THE WIND? THE BIRDS CHIRPING?
I THINK SO.
WHOOOOOOOSH!
CHIRP CHIRP!
NOW TAKE A DEEP BREATH AND PLAY.

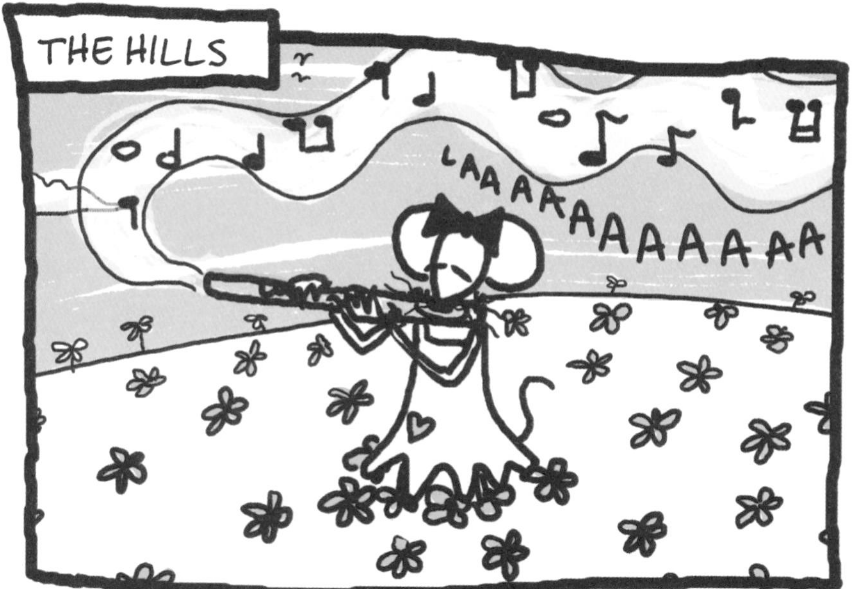
THE HILLS
LAAAAAAAAAAAAAA

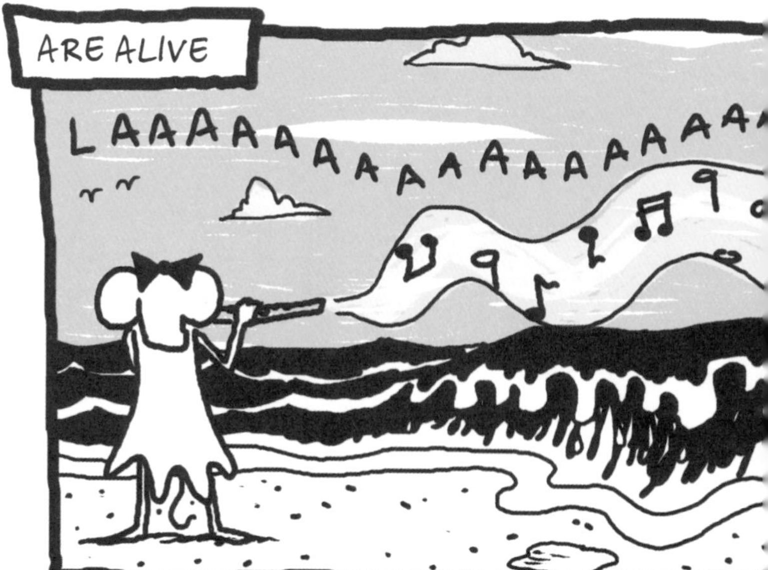
ARE ALIVE
LAAAAAAAAAAAAAAAAAA

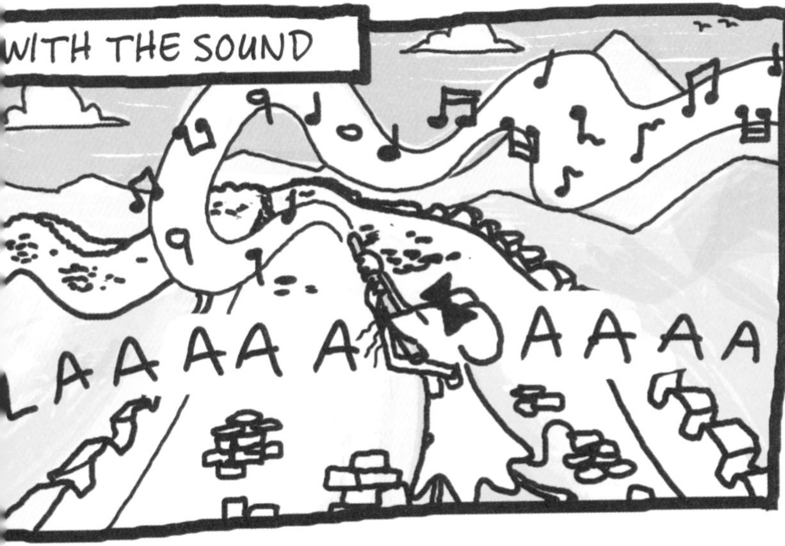
WITH THE SOUND
LAAAAA AAAAA

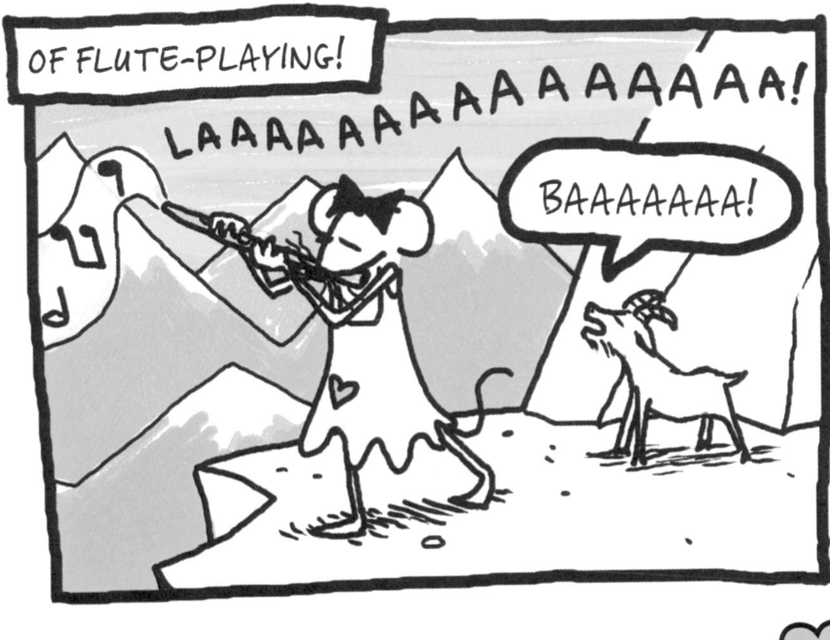
OF FLUTE-PLAYING!
LAAAAAAAAAAAAAAA!
BAAAAAAA!

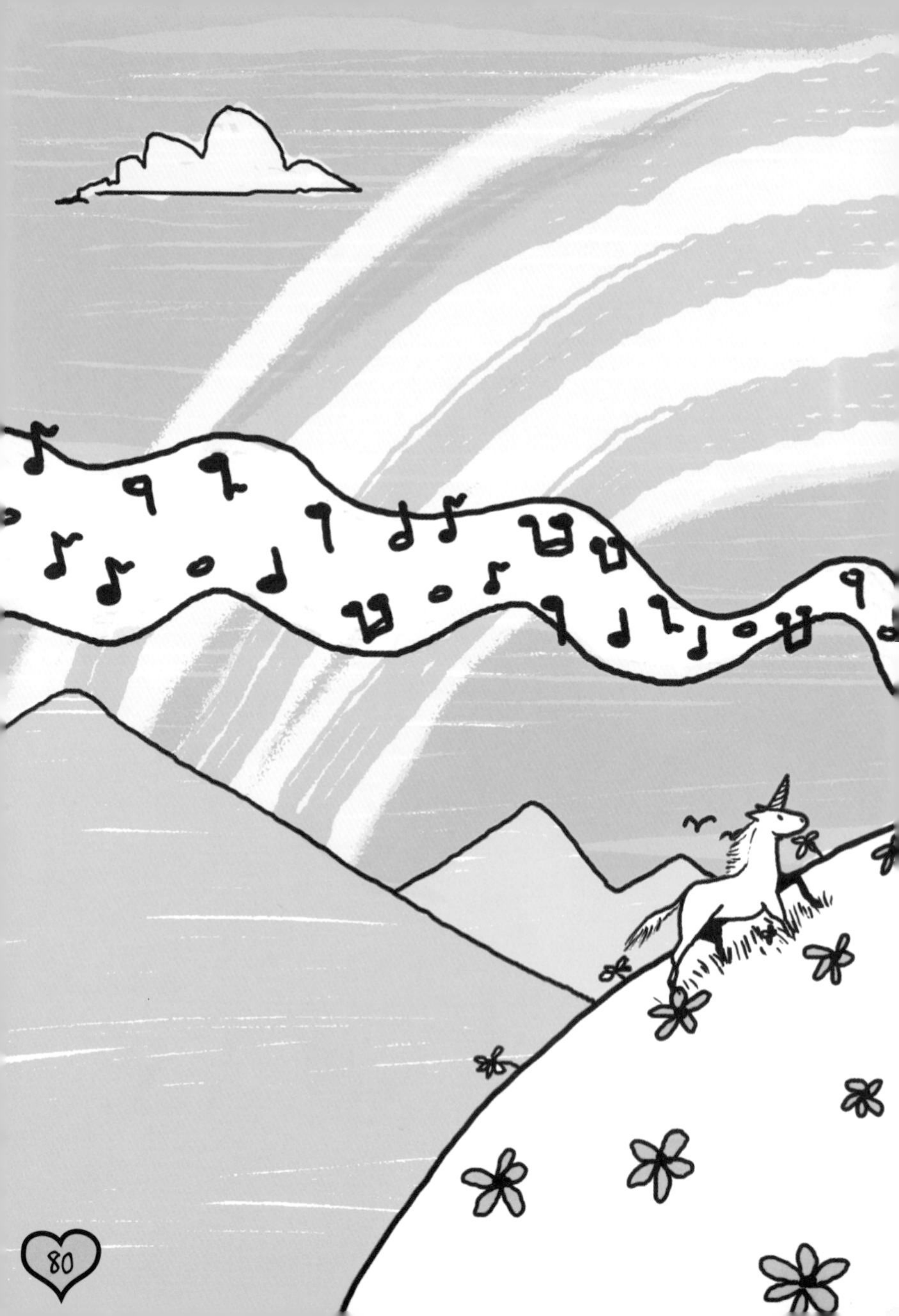

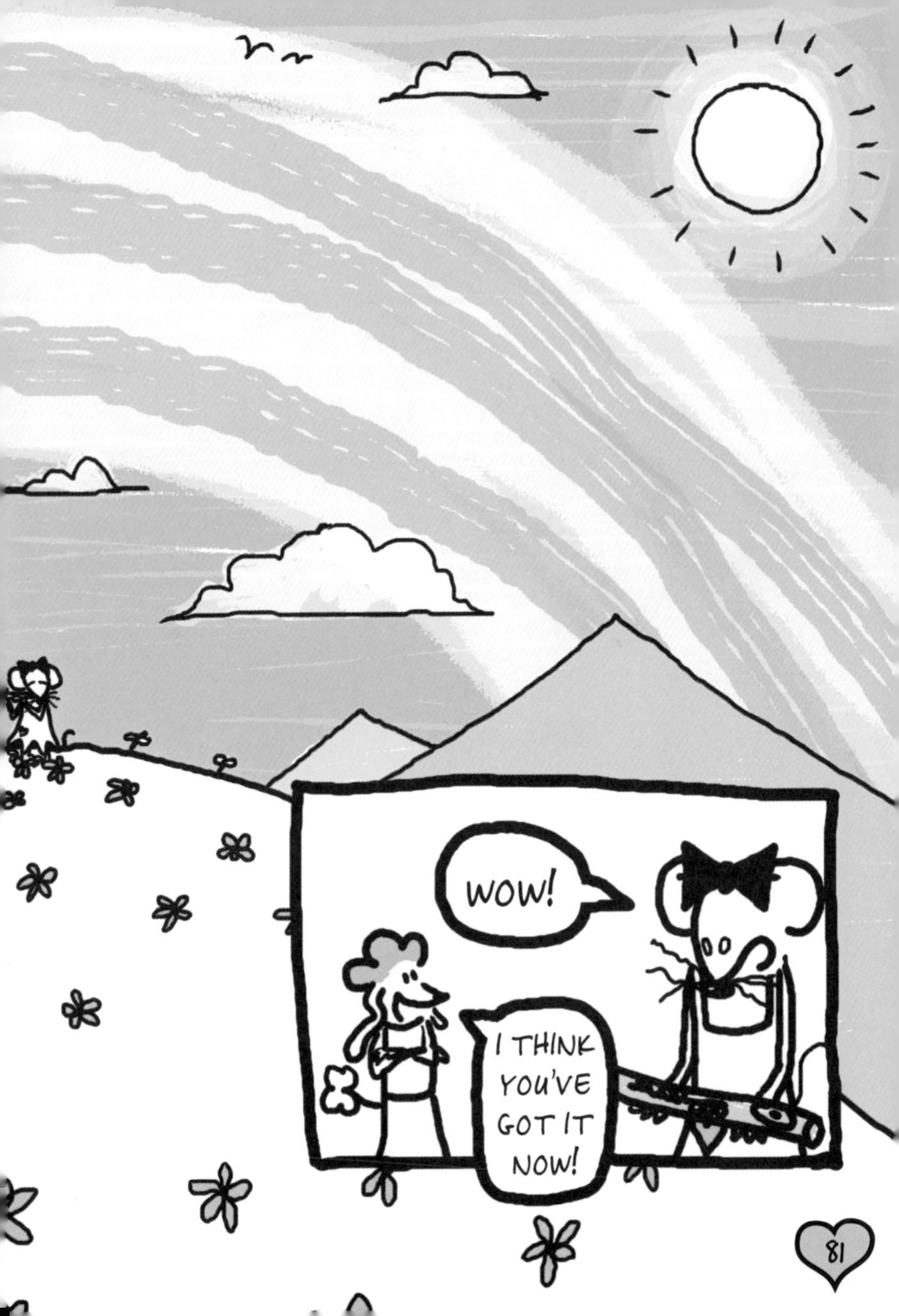
WOW!
I THINK YOU'VE GOT IT NOW!

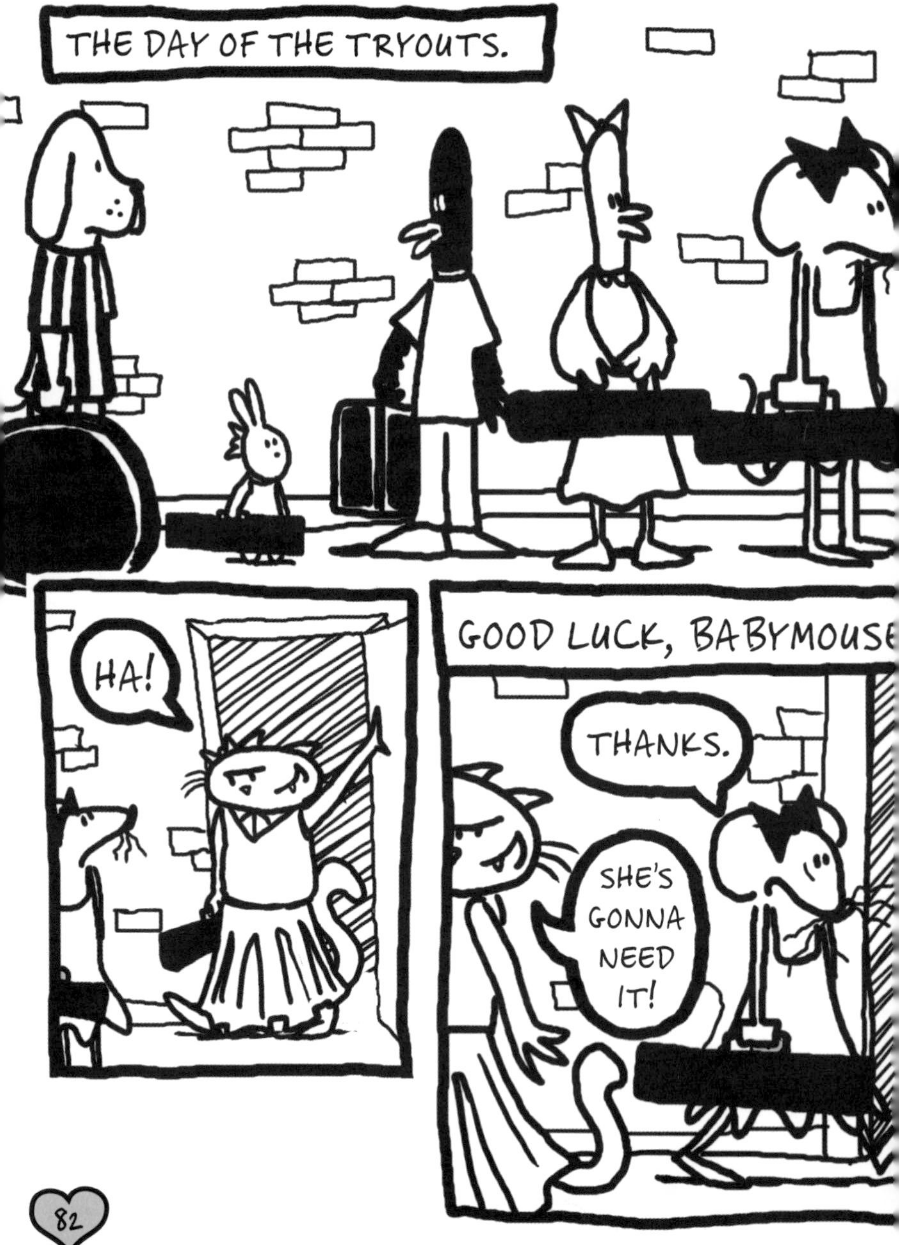

THE DAY OF THE TRYOUTS.
HA!
GOOD LUCK, BABYMOUSE
THANKS.
SHE'S GONNA NEED IT!

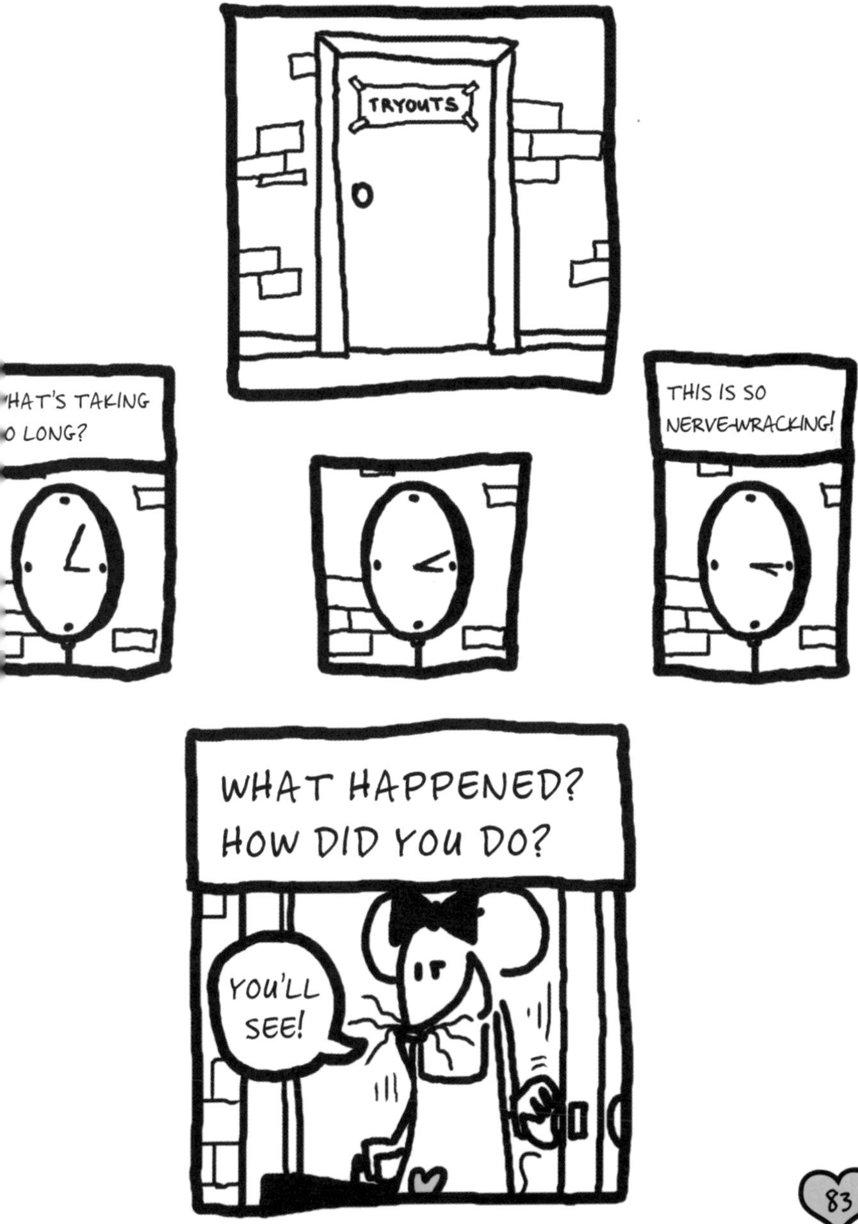
TRYOUTS
HAT'S TAKING
O LONG?
THIS IS SO
NERVE-WRACKING!
WHAT HAPPENED?
HOW DID YOU DO?
YOU'LL
SEE!

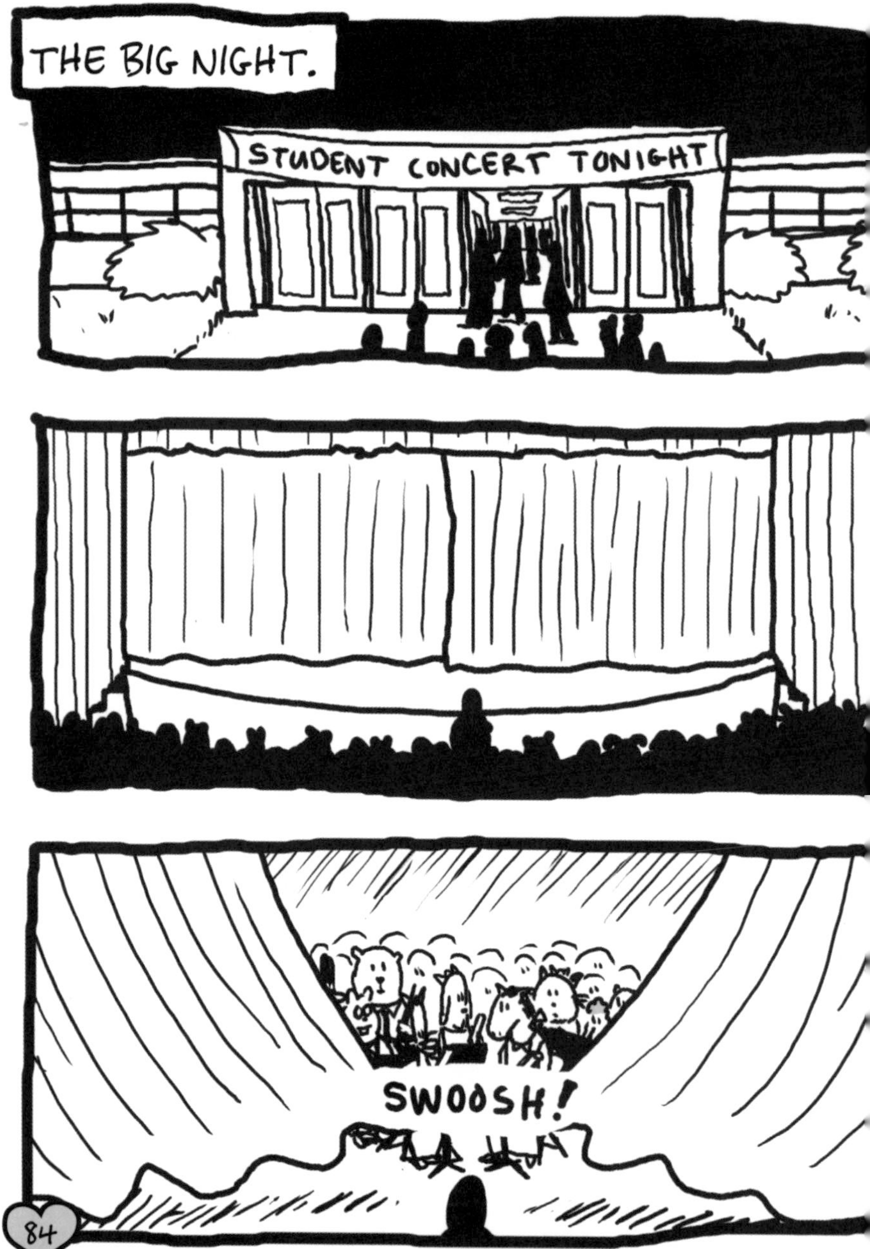
THE BIG NIGHT.
STUDENT CONCERT TONIGHT
SWOOSH!

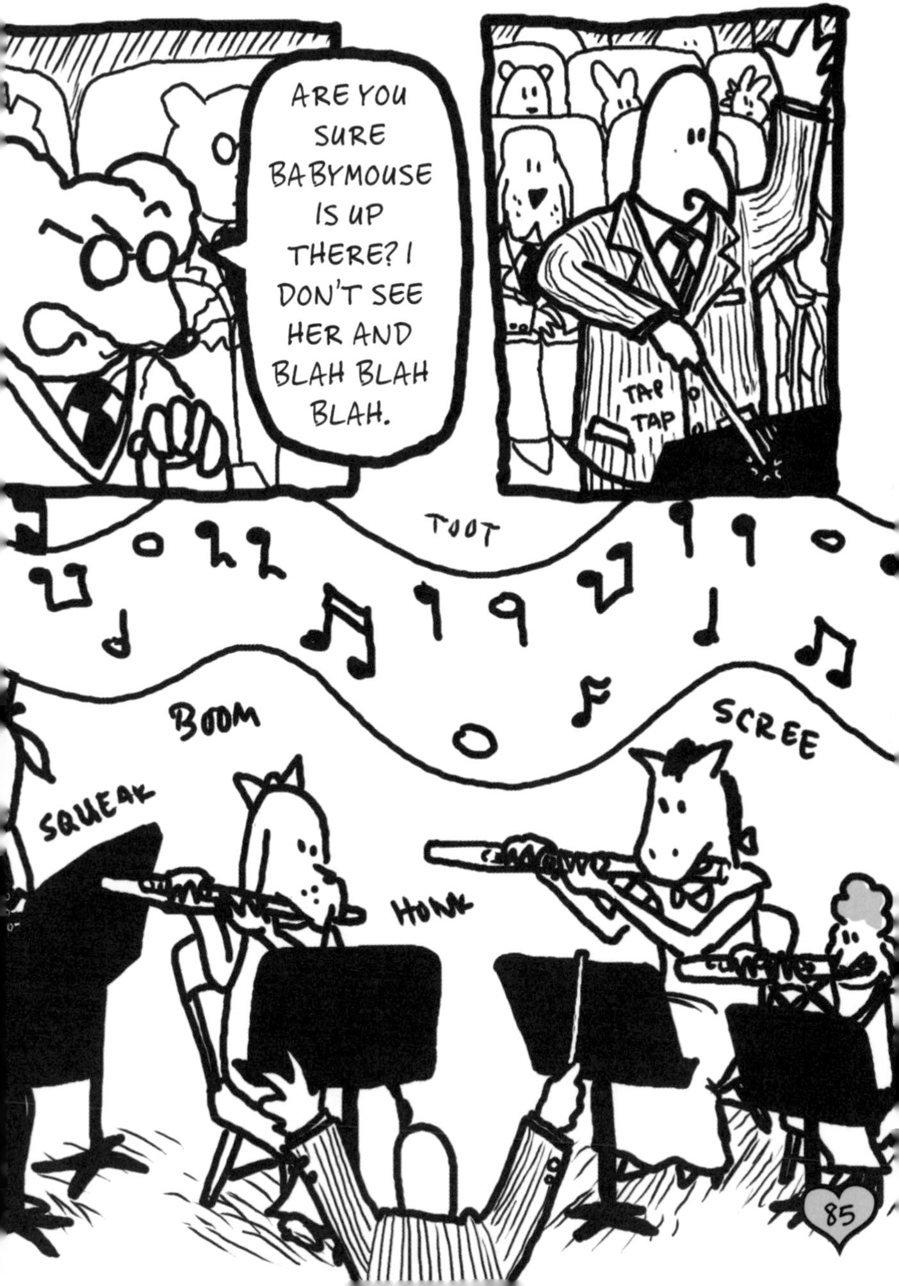
ARE YOU SURE BABYMOUSE IS UP THERE? I DON'T SEE HER AND BLAH BLAH BLAH.
TAP TAP
TOOT
BOOM
SCREE
SQUEAK
HONK

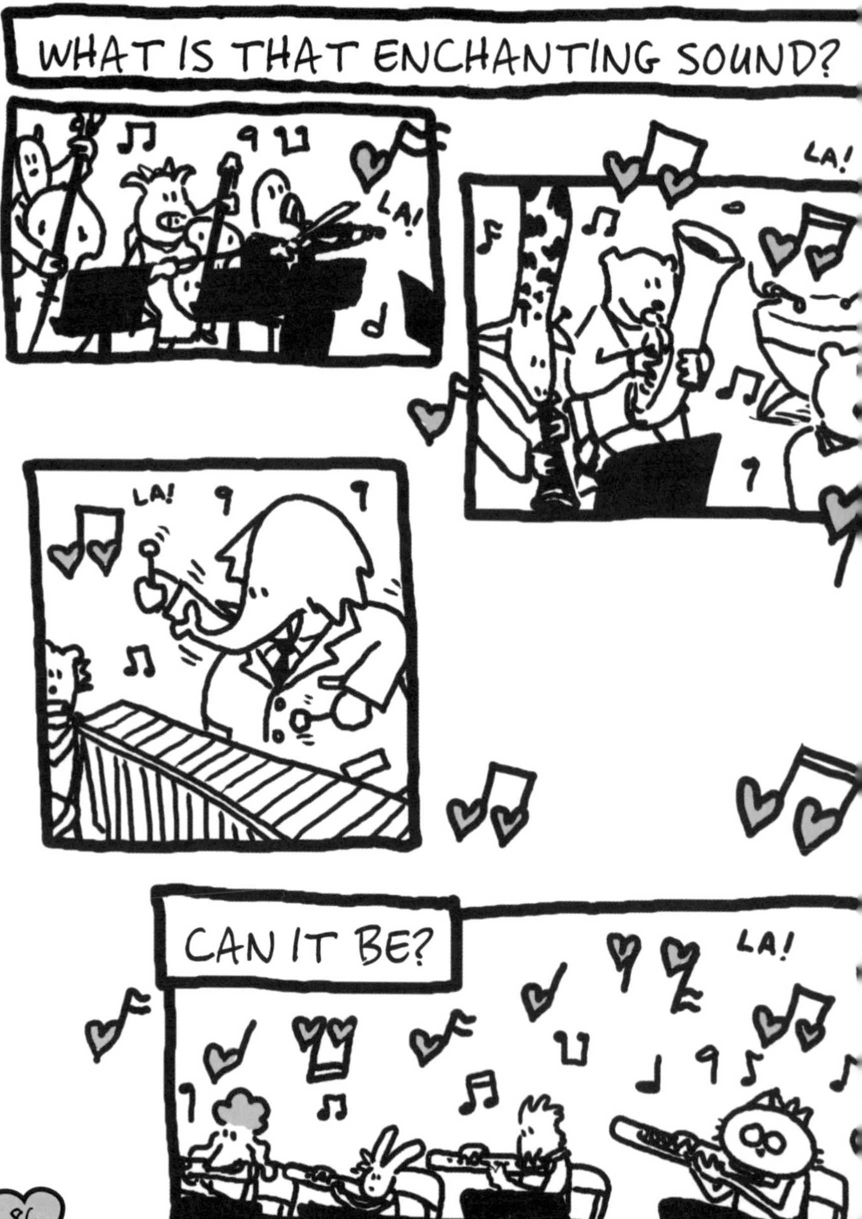
WHAT IS THAT ENCHANTING SOUND?
LA!
LA!
LA!
CAN IT BE?
LA!

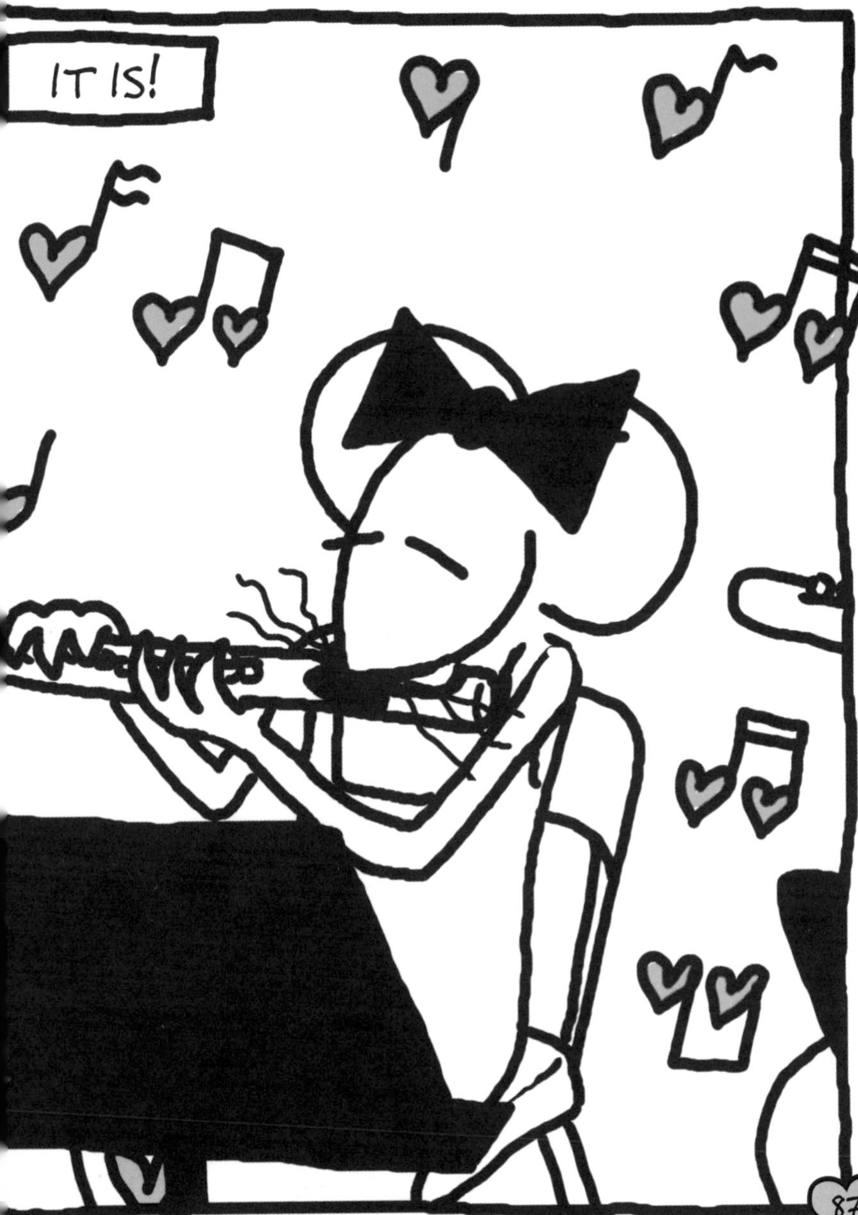
IT IS!

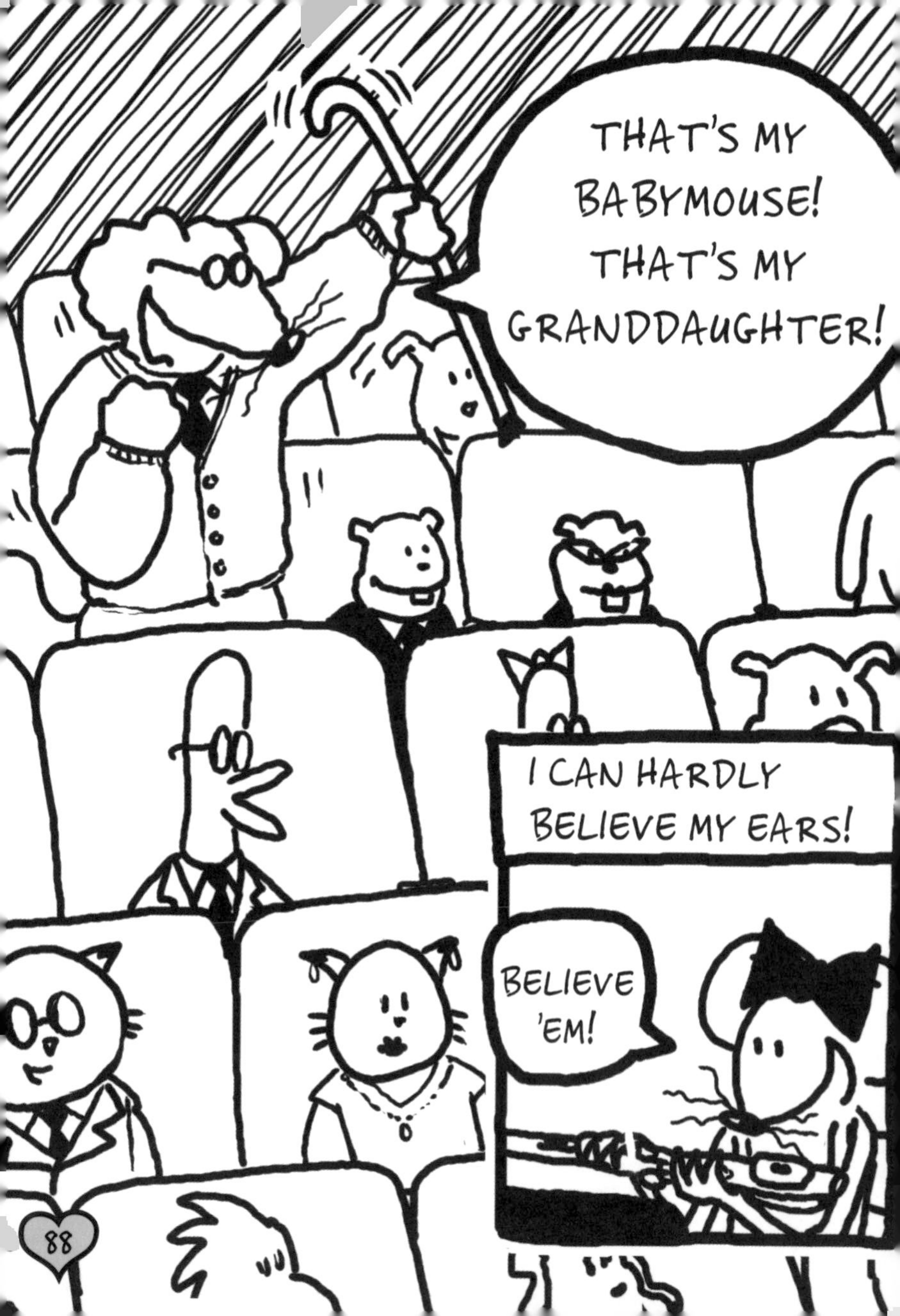
THAT'S MY BABYMOUSE! THAT'S MY GRANDDAUGHTER!
I CAN HARDLY BELIEVE MY EARS!
BELIEVE 'EM!

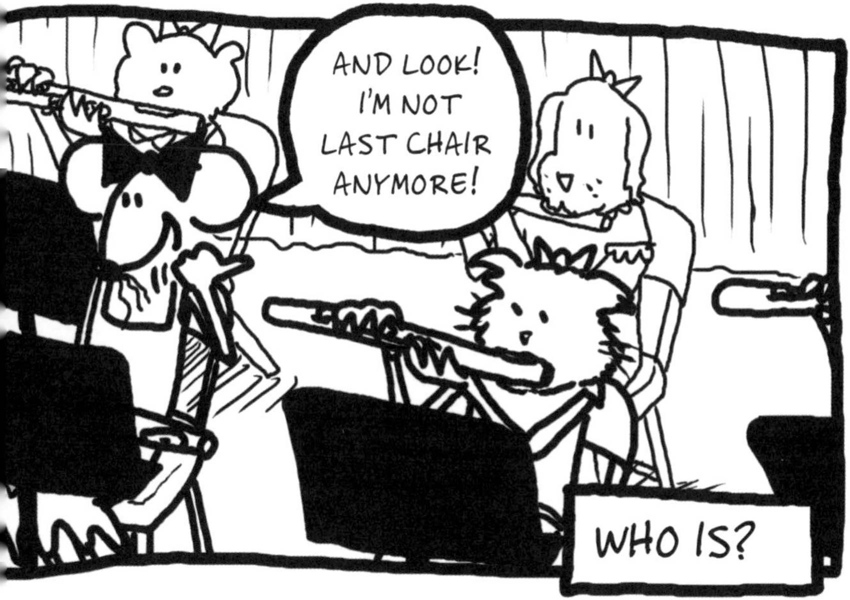
AND LOOK! I'M NOT LAST CHAIR ANYMORE!
WHO IS?

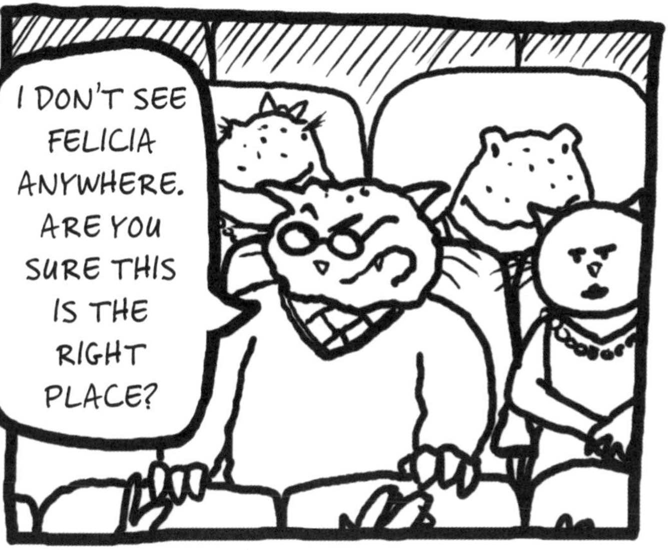
I DON'T SEE FELICIA ANYWHERE. ARE YOU SURE THIS IS THE RIGHT PLACE?

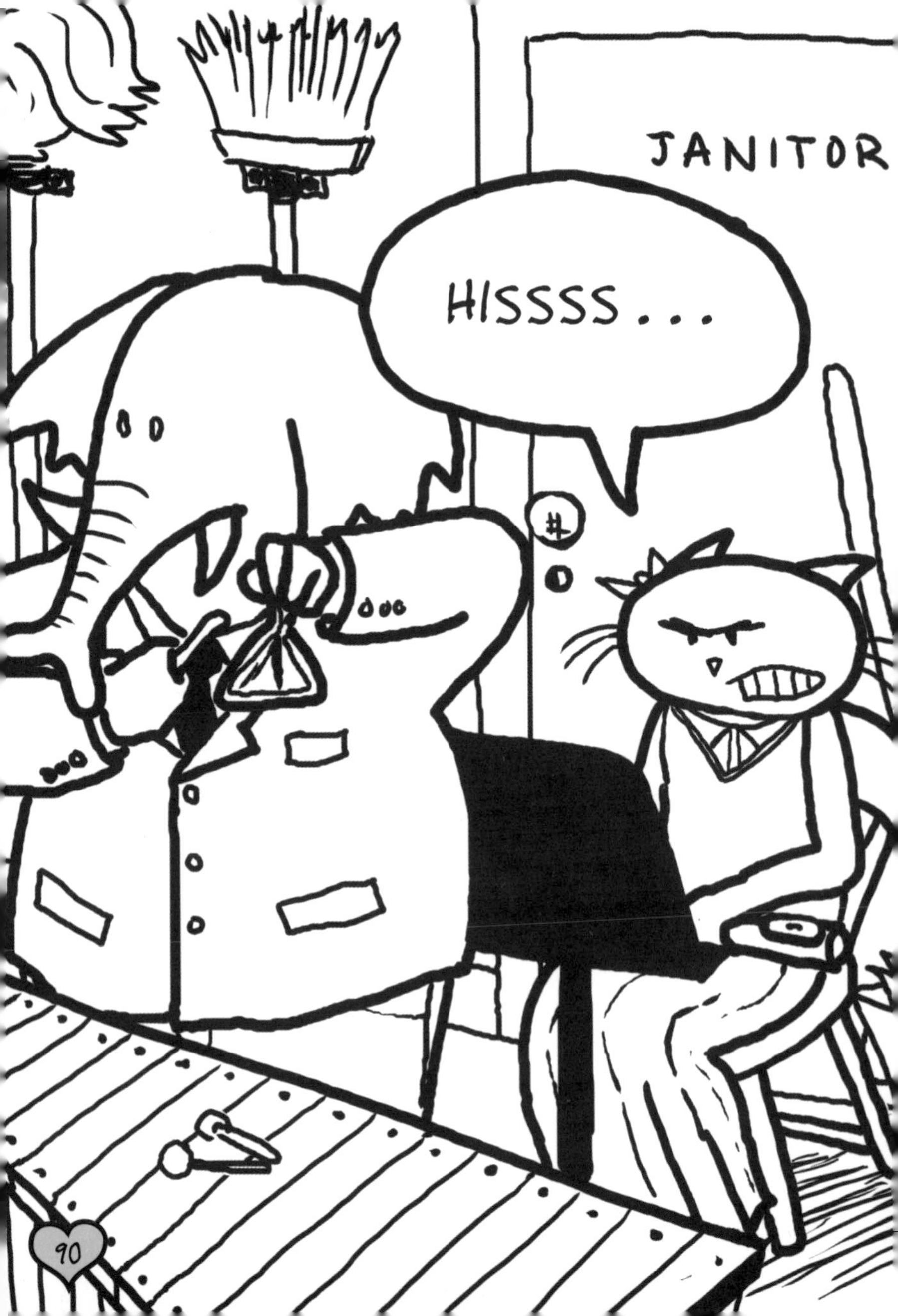
JANITOR
HISSSS...

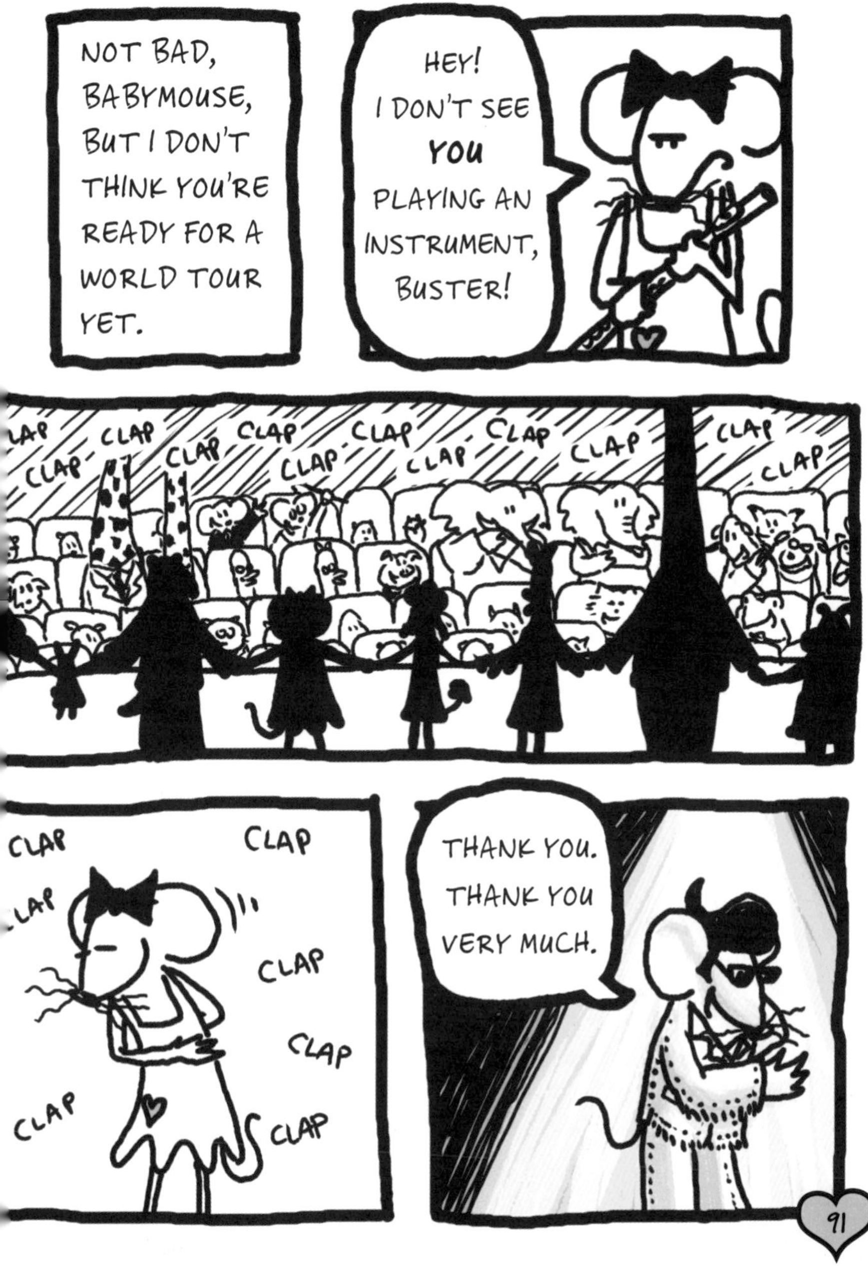
NOT BAD, BABYMOUSE, BUT I DON'T THINK YOU'RE READY FOR A WORLD TOUR YET.
HEY! I DON'T SEE **YOU** PLAYING AN INSTRUMENT, BUSTER!
CLAP CLAP CLAP CLAP CLAP CLAP CLAP CLAP CLAP CLAP CLAP CLAP
CLAP CLAP CLAP CLAP CLAP CLAP CLAP
THANK YOU. THANK YOU VERY MUCH.

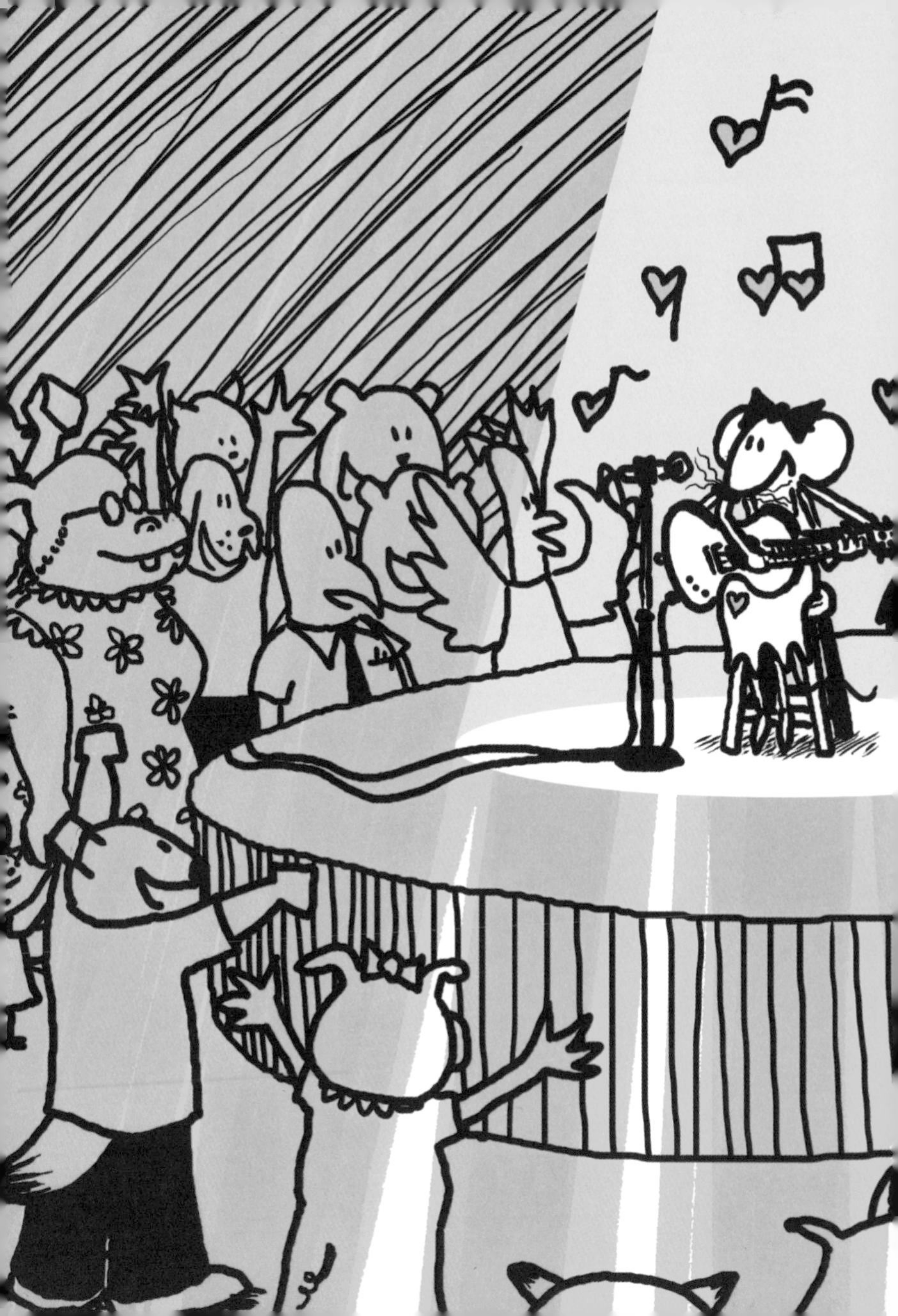

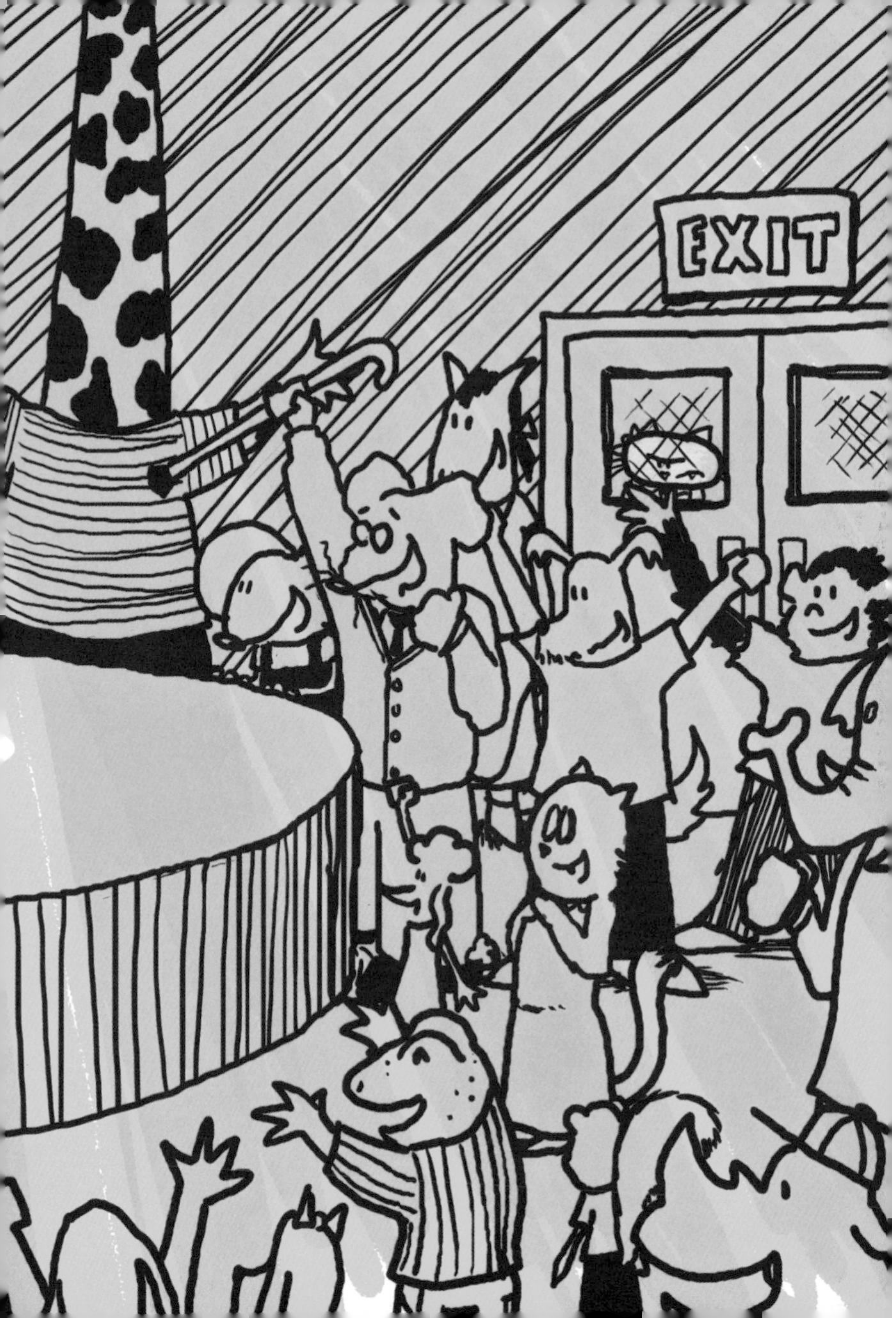
EXIT

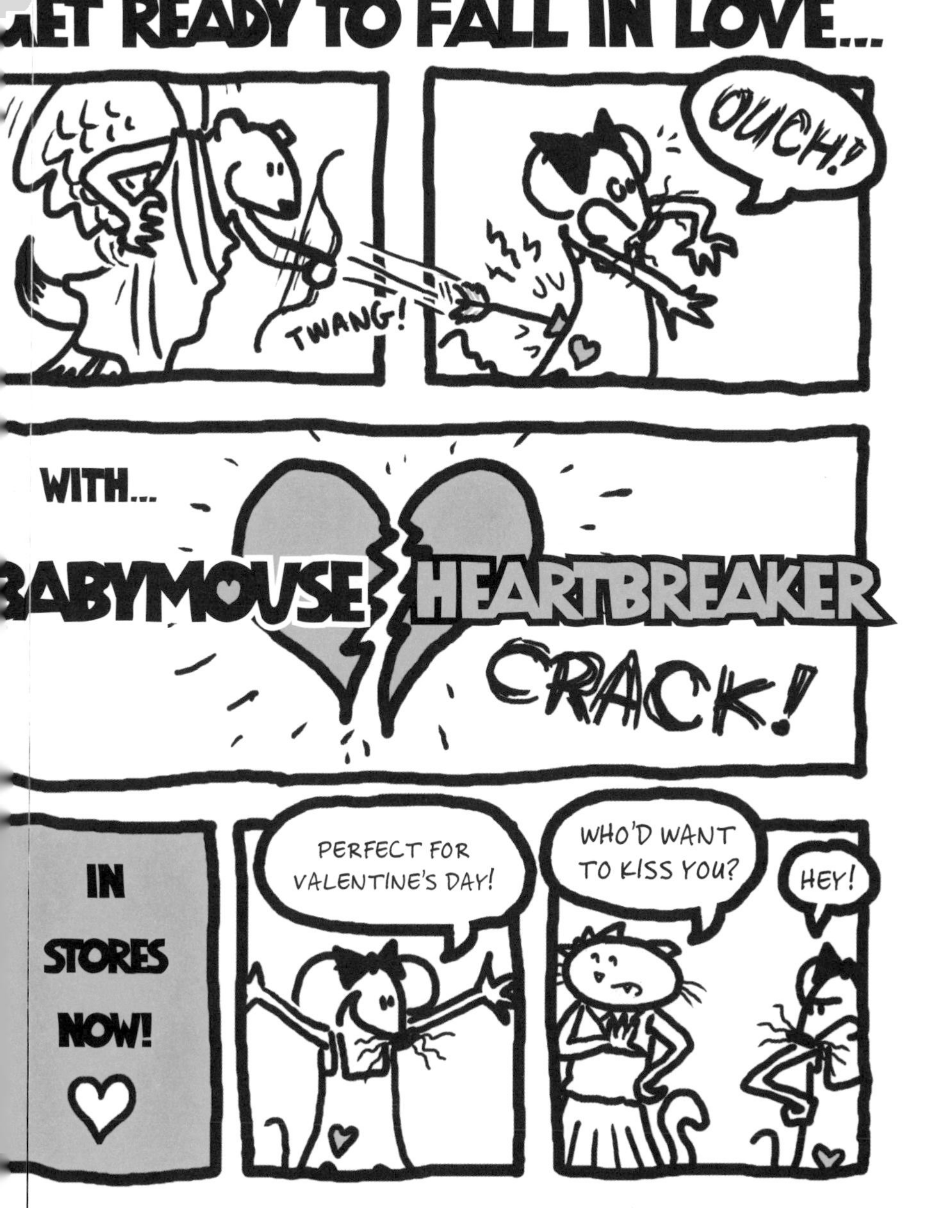
GET READY TO FALL IN LOVE...
TWANG!
OUCH!
WITH...
BABYMOUSE HEARTBREAKER
CRACK!
IN STORES NOW!
PERFECT FOR VALENTINE'S DAY!
WHO'D WANT TO KISS YOU?
HEY!

BABYMOUSE BONUS!

• TIPS ON BEING A ROCK STAR •

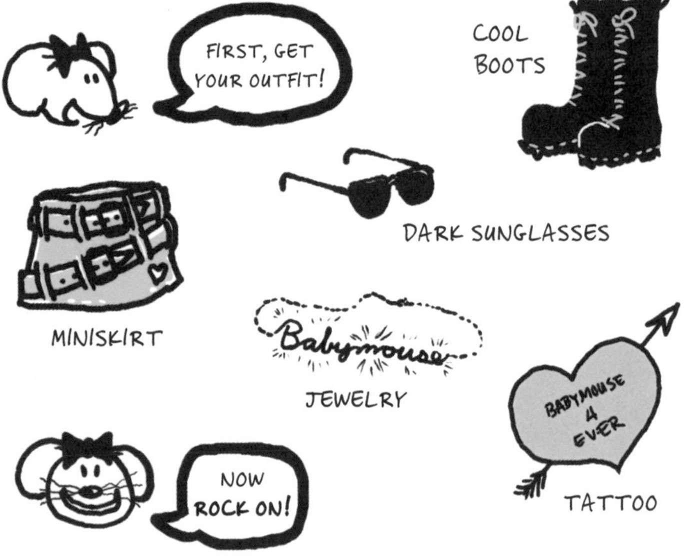

FIRST, GET YOUR OUTFIT!
COOL BOOTS
DARK SUNGLASSES
MINISKIRT
Babymouse
JEWELRY
BABYMOUSE 4 EVER
TATTOO
NOW ROCK ON!

BE MYSTERIOUS! BE DEMANDING! BE A DIVA!

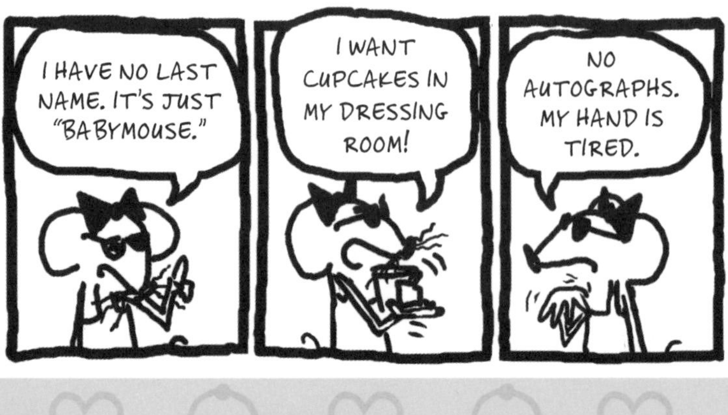

I HAVE NO LAST NAME. IT'S JUST "BABYMOUSE."
I WANT CUPCAKES IN MY DRESSING ROOM!
NO AUTOGRAPHS. MY HAND IS TIRED.